Other Titles By
Loure Bussey

Secretly In Love

Tropical Heat

Love So True

Most of All

Images of Ecstasy

If Loving You Is Wrong

Twist of Fate

A Feeling Like No Other

Nightfall

Dangerous Passions

Just The Thought Of You

A Taste Of Love

If Loving You Is Wrong

Please Visit

LoureBussey.com

Kiss Me All Over

Loure Bussey

Parker Publishing, LLC
www.Parker-Publishing.com

Noire Passion is an imprint of Parker Publishing, LLC.

Copyright © 2007 by Loure Bussey

Published by Parker Publishing, LLC
12523 Limonite Ave. Suite #440-438
Mira Loma, CA 91752
www.parker-publishing.com

ISBN: 978-1-60043-033-6

First Edition
Manufactured in the U.S.A.
Printed by Bang Printing, Brainerd, MN

Dedication

To Brandon Christopher, You are the love of my life

Chapter One

When Amara Hart slipped off her white, silk kimono, revealing her nude, shimmering body to the classroom full of artists, her heart sped and her limbs quivered. Her financial situation caused her to do something she never imagined. However, when she spotted her ex-lover's best friend and business partner, Bryce Davidson, among the art students, her embarrassment soared to another level. She had thought of him much more than she should have and never in her wildest dreams imagined that he would be a student in the class.

Tempted to grab her cover up and flee, Amara could barely pose on the cold table in the gracefully sensuous manner the instructor requested. Each time her wide, slanted-up eyes dared to wander among the night class, they immediately captured Bryce. His dazzling, dark eyes met hers, making her wonder what he thought of her new occupation. She just knew he would tell her ex-boyfriend, Terrence, about her pursuits.

At the wind up of the class, the teacher and many of the students thanked Amara for posing. Acknowledging their gratitude, she forced a smile, and turned around to grab her kimono. The flimsy fabric embellished a dull, wooden chair.

While tying the sash, she suddenly inhaled a trace of spicy cologne. Footsteps approached her from the rear. Sensing the tall presence behind her, Amara wished she hadn't bothered to lace the sash, but raced out of the room the instant the class ended.

"Amara," a deep, sexy voice called, floating beyond her shoulders.

Brushing back long, cinnamon colored curls from her face Amara turned around and once again faced Bryce's magnetic eyes. They complimented pudding-smooth, rich chocolate skin, a gently sloped nose, and a strong jaw. A neat, black, narrow line of hair edged the latter connecting with a silky mustache, which circled the most inviting lips. Close-cropped, dark, wavy hair framed his face. The handsome features crowned a body formed with broad shoulders, cantaloupe-sized muscles, a tapered waist, and powerfully built legs.

Amara thought Bryce's black, velvet sweat suit showed off his well-built physique all too well. But it wasn't the first time she viewed him this way. In the days following her breakup with Terrence, each time her ex's best friend crossed her path in the office, a rush of heat flowed through her body. As he stood before her now, the sensation teased her again.

"Hi," she said, much calmer than she felt.

Bryce flashed a broad, mesmerizing smile, which always made the women at her former job melt. "How are you doing?"

"I'm fine."

"It's nice to see you again. I miss seeing you at the office. I didn't know you were a model."

She shrugged. "It's something new for me."

"So you're no longer a real estate agent?"

Amara hesitated; her answer would have meant dredging up drama that made this year one of the most wretched times of her life. She glanced at the last of the class, which left the room rather than respond to him. "I better get going."

"Do you need a ride home?"

"No, but thanks, my car is in the parking lot. See you around."

Amara fled into the changing room where her jeans, top, shoes, purse, bra, and panties were. She felt badly about her abruptness with Bryce, but she couldn't tell him her problems. On top of everything else, this first night of bare skinned modeling had been difficult for her. Spotting him among those who scrutinized her bare flesh made it worse. Of all people to behold and sketch her naked, why did it have to be her ex-man's business partner and best friend?

She had met Bryce three weeks before her dismissal from TJ Realty Corporation. At the same time, she had broken up with her boss and lover, Terrence Johnson. She heard from another agent that an Illinoisan, Bryce Davidson, had moved to Maryland to become a partner in TJ Realty after Terrence's accountant mismanaged his taxes. It led to costly fines, which ultimately downsized the company. Bryce owned two other mega successful businesses in Chicago. When asked to assist his old college buddy with resurrecting his once thriving enterprise, Bryce did not hesitate.

He partnered with Terrence, making a substantial financial investment, offering business savvy, and bringing with him key contacts. Although, Amara hadn't known him long or well, she watched him uplift the company's morale. Unlike their distaste for Terrence, the employees liked Bryce. He was down-to-earth and respectful toward everybody, including Terrence. What's more, the women drooled at his drop-dead gorgeous looks.

After dressing, Amara walked into the university parking lot and soon plopped onto her car's worn, leather cushions. Mentally, she replayed her nude modeling experience and wished she'd never have to do it again. Accepting that she had no other choice, she took a deep breath and stuck her key in the ignition. Her old beat up jalopy of a car wouldn't start. She turned on the headlights and repeatedly turned the key. The engine wouldn't turn over. Resting her face on the steering wheel, she had no idea what to do.

A knock on the half-open driver's window startled her. Swaying back from the glass, Amara's eyes leveled on the face. Bryce's unexpected warm gaze eased her. There had been a few muggings on the campus lately and she was relieved that a robber wasn't attempting to prey upon her.

"Having a problem?" he asked.

"A big one. I knew this car was on its way out, but I didn't expect it to conk out tonight. I need it for work and to see my brother. Now, I'm so screwed."

He pointed at the gauge. "You checked the gas?"

"I filled it up this morning."

Rubbing his chin, he speculated. "And it's not the battery

5

because the headlights wouldn't be on. Why don't you let me give it a try?"

"You wouldn't mind?"

"Of course not." He gripped the door handle.

"I appreciate this." Amara unlocked the door and scooted into the passenger seat.

Instantly, spicy cologne lightly filled the air. The scent reminded her of what she used to admire about Bryce and his casual attitude. He settled in beside her and attempted to get her clunker moving. Having his strong, masculine presence so close, a feeling of comfort came over her despite the humiliation she endured around him earlier. When he stepped out of the car and raised its hood, she felt more grateful of his offer to help her.

Rejoining her in the car, Bryce didn't look hopeful. "I know a little bit about cars since I used to work on them with my dad. You need to get this one to a shop. You might even need to get a new car."

"Oh, no," Pursing her full lips, Amara stared ahead beyond the glass into the parking lot, which became darker and emptier with each minute.

She lacked the funds for car repairs or a new car. She barely had enough money for food, let alone the rent she owed for her apartment. Today her modeling assignment just began, so she couldn't count on income from it for the next few weeks. And once she did receive it, could she make an adequate partial payment for the overdue amount on her brother's medical care?

Suddenly aware of Bryce staring at her, Amara turned her head to catch his dark brown eyes roaming over her body, and then swiftly meeting her gaze. "I know what you're thinking about me." Her eyes narrowed at him.

Bryce shifted, turning toward her with a mysterious twinkle in his eyes. "You do? Tell me then."

"You're thinking I'm trash for taking off my clothes for money."

Faintly, Bryce shook his head. "You're wrong."

"No, I'm not. You're thinking this sistah went from selling half million dollar homes to taking it all off for whatever she could get."

"No way was I thinking that." He grasped her hand, squeezing t gently.

The touch surprised her. So did the intensity in his eyes. Each stirred something within her. They made her acutely aware of a rush of heat that flowed in her body. "I hope I don't sound out of line because of your prior relationship with Terrence," Bryce said, "but when I sketched you in class, I thought you're a striking artist's model and a woman taking care of herself. And from what Terrence told me, you're also a sister taking care of a brother who was hurt badly in a skiing accident. There is nothing trashy about that. In fact, it's to be admired."

A hint of a smile tugged the corners of Amara's lips. "Thank you."

"Well, that's how I feel about it."

Silence and stares lingered between them. Reluctantly, Bryce let go of Amara's hand. She peered beyond the front window again and her heart felt lighter than it had before. She noticed only a van and truck remained in the parking lot. "I think I'm going to leave my car here tonight and handle everything tomorrow."

Bryce frowned. "You sure? I can get my mechanic to take a look at it right now if you want."

"I appreciate the offer. I really do. But I'll leave it here."

"All right. I guess it should be safe here with security around. I'll take you home…if you don't mind."

Amara smiled softly. "I don't mind. Thank you."

"It's my pleasure."

"So what made you take the art class?" Amara asked Bryce as he wheeled his silver Mercedes-Benz down the brightly lit, four lane avenue. Several cars whizzed by before she switched her interest to his attractive profile. "Is it something to do to spice up your life?"

Keeping his eyes on the road, Bryce grinned. "In a way, I guess. I've always loved drawing since I was a kid. A childhood friend really turned me on to it. We used to say we would be artists when we grew up. And she did."

"That's nice."

"One night, recently, I dreamed about her. She told me to get back into art. She used to tell me I was good at it. Drawing and painting relaxes and excites me at the same time. She understood my passion for it." He smiled and appeared faraway. "We used to have some good times."

Amara grew intrigued because of a change in his facial expression. It was evident this childhood friend had become something more to him. Though, he seemed to imply that she was part of his past. "So, it sounds like you haven't been in touch with this friend lately to tell her about the dream or your art class."

Bryce didn't respond immediately. He looked ahead at the avenue, his sparkling eyes blinking rapidly. Finally, he said, "No, I can't tell her. She passed away."

"Oh." Amara looked out the window at the sunset and avoided expressing a traditional sorrowful reply. Expressions of condolences reminded her of her parents' deaths in a head-on collision, caused by a drunk driver. She'd been a sophomore in college at the time. Thereafter, she became guardian of her younger brother, Derrick, and they bonded closer than ever. Amara loved him so much that she often wondered if it compared to the love a mother felt for a child. She lived to make him feel loved, happy, and safe.

"Do you think you'll still be nervous for the second class?" Bryce asked after a long period of silence. A bit of mischief flickered over his face with the question. It was a different expression than the one he had when he mentioned his childhood friend.

"Who said I was nervous?" Amara asked.

"I do, I saw it."

"You saw wrong," she quipped with a quick laugh.

"You trembled." Bryce glanced at her, and then focused back on the shadowy streets of her neighborhood. "I certainly saw trembling."

"If you did, it was because I had nothing on and was chilly."

"How could you be chilly with that sweat making your body look so slick like that?"

"Excuse me?" Amara uttered, raising her waxed brows. Was he

calling her nasty and sweaty?

"I mean your skin had this sultry shimmer, a glow, almost like…"

Tilting her head, she gazed at him curiously. "Like what?"

"Like when a woman is aroused and turned on. It made for a very seductive portrait."

"Is that right?"

"Oh, yes. It's just too bad the portrait will never capture the true essence, no matter how skilled the artist is."

"What do you mean?"

"I mean no one can capture that trembling I saw in your legs and thighs." Pausing, Bryce's Adam's apple bobbed and he swallowed. "And your…"

"My what?" she asked, excited by his words and actions, but trying not to show it.

"I don't want to get out of line."

"You're not. We're having a conversation about art."

"All right then. Your….your breasts, they shook as your chest rose and fell with your heartbeat." Again, his Adam's apple moved and Bryce swallowed. "No artist can capture all of that in a portrait."

Tense silence filled the air during the rest of the car ride to her home. Chewing a Hershey's chocolate kiss Bryce had given her, Amara did everything she could to keep her eyes from drifting back to his face and body. She wondered if all his small talk about her posing nude was his way of flirting. She wondered if he could detect her attraction toward him. On the other hand, what if Bryce had spoke to her simply from an artist's perspective?

The mental inquiry halted once his silvery vehicle approached her apartment doorstep. At that instant, she panicked. Every one of Amara's belongings sat on the lawn of the attractive four-family complex where she lived.

She grabbed her head. "Oh, my God! They threw me out!"

With her heart racing, Amara hopped out of Bryce's sports coupe before he could finish parking. As she flitted moved among her possessions, she questioned why had so many bad things happened to her? She caught a several neighbors from down the street huddled together, gawking in her direction. Most likely, the eviction crew removed her furnishings from her apartment in bright daylight and the spectacle drew an audience. Trying to ignore them, Amara rushed into the building and up the stairwell to her second floor apartment.

A padlock prevented her entrance with an eviction notice stuck to the door. Amara received daily letters from the property owner threatening eviction if she didn't pay the past due rent. She returned the letters explaining her thorny circumstances, but withheld the details of what Terrence did to her. At first, along with the returned letters, she had sent small payments towards her past-due rent. However, she came to a point when she could no longer pay anything. Now, at thirty-four years old, she was homeless.

By the time Bryce caught up with her in front of the bolted apartment door, Amara couldn't meet his gaze. She looked in every direction to avoid him. Not only did she feel embarrassed, but also she felt tears welling up in her eyes. She couldn't appear weak. She couldn't let him see her fall apart. Lately, it felt like if she began crying about her troubles, she would never stop.

Amara blinked back tears and struggled to still her quivering lips. Despite her efforts, before she knew anything she became helpless against the warm tears sliding down her cheeks, seeping beyond her lips, forcing its salty taste on her tongue. Finally facing Bryce's frown, she opened her mouth to ask if the property owner's actions were legal. Didn't she have rights, too? And what if thieves had rummaged through her things and stolen her precious possessions? However, the questions she wanted to pose to him strangled among the emotion caught in her throat.

"Don't worry." His voice was a deep, soothing whisper.

Amara sniffled. "But I don't know what I'm going to do."

"I do. I'll call a moving service, and we'll have your things moved into one of the garages at my house within a few hours."

"I can't do that to you."

"You're not doing anything to me." Bryce grasped her hand and caressed it. "You're not inconveniencing me in any way."

"But…" she uttered, feeling comforted by his gentle touch.

"I insist. You're going to stay at my place tonight. I have a large house with plenty of spare rooms."

"I can't pay the movers."

"I'll take care of it."

Amara studied him. Furrows formed between his black, mink-like brows, while his tall, muscular physique leaned forward as if prepared to embrace or catch her if she collapsed. And God knows she wanted to collapse. She wanted to feel his broad, strong chest and just hold on, hold on to …someone who made her feel safe and protected.

She managed a tiny smile in spite of her tears. "Thank you, Bryce."

"I'm glad I can help."

"And I promise—I promise to repay you." Of course she would return his money, but along with it, she wanted to do something even greater for him.

"Don't worry about that. Just let me take care of everything."

Amara looked at him, amazed. "I can't get over you doing this for me."

"Why does it surprise you?"

"Because we don't know that much about each other." But even as she said those words, she couldn't deny that something about him made her feel connected with him.

Bryce stared in her eyes for a long time. "Are you sure about that? Sometimes people don't have to know each other a long time or even know everything about another person to know them. We just feel what they feel." His dark eyes lowered and he gazed at her lips.

Chapter Two

Lusty pulsations at the base of Amara's stomach teased her. The sensation grew with every second Bryce stared at her mouth. Somehow, his stare even caressed her body. Warmth spread through her and the pulses in her lower belly progressed to throbbing between her thighs.

Amara surrendered to temptation and became obsessed with Bryce's mouth, as well. Even in the midst of her enormous predicament, she wondered how greedily his lips could sip the sweetness from hers and if his tongue could thrust in her mouth so seductively that she would be wet and aching for his loving. Bryce looked that good. He was being so sweet to her. She could only imagine the heights of arousal he could take her to, to ease her pain. Every sexy thing about him assured her he was a passionate kisser. Then again, so was another man who tasted her lips and all else in what seemed like another lifetime.

With reality dawning on her, Amara looked away from Bryce. As if he too had realized Terrence's presence was with them even if he was nowhere in sight, Bryce cleared his throat.

"So I'll make that call to the movers now."

"Okay."

Bryce pulled a cell phone out of his sweat pants pocket. Within an hour, moving men had loaded her possessions on their truck.

Hours later, Amara strolled through a cozy, Spanish Mediterranean style mansion. Adorned with earth tones, hardwood floors, and a stylish blend of antique and modern furnishings, she felt as if she wandered within a page of a home design magazine.

Gazing up at the high domed ceilings, she gasped, "Wow."

"I guess that means you like it." Bryce stood back with his arms folded.

"Ooh, you just don't know how much. One of the last homes I sold was in this style. I had hoped to buy one for my brother and myself. "

"You won't just hope. You'll do it. But for now, I hope you like the room you will be staying in."

After Bryce escorted Amara up a staircase, she found herself in the only room decorated with carpet. The rug, pecan colored and smelling freshly shampooed, blended soothingly with the vanilla colored walls and soft, beige furnishings. When she finished drooling at the décor, her lips curled in a sensuous smile.

"Do you like?" He flashed a tantalizing grin right back at her.

"Oh, I more than like. Thank you. Tonight could have been my worst nightmare if not for you."

"Well, it wasn't. Now get some sleep."

"I'll try."

Amara admired his tall, powerfully built physique as he strode out of the room and closed the door. Collapsing backwards on the bed with her arms outstretched, she gazed at the ceiling and thought about him. Bryce Davidson had been her angel tonight. More than once, she had restrained the urge to throw her arms around his broad shoulders and show her gratefulness. She knew that would have been wrong, because of who Terrence was to Bryce, and who he once was to her.

Not only was Terence Johnson one of the most illustrious businessmen in Crystal Falls, Maryland, but one of the most sexy, gorgeous, and charismatic creatures Amara had ever encountered. Even so, when Amara began working as a real estate agent at his firm, she hadn't planned on letting him seduce her. Neither had she planned on them having a nine-month love affair more passionate than any she had ever experienced before.

Friends warned her not to romantically entangle herself with a colleague, and heaven forbid, her boss. Nevertheless, how could they understand the loneliness that consumed her prior to meeting Terrence, compared with the sensually alive feeling that filled her when he whisked her into his life? The magic he brought to her world made up for past heartbreak and loneliness.

Once Amara learned Terrence had a wife secretly tucked away

in a mental institution in North Carolina, her trust in her former lover shattered. Moreover, Amara began to suspect that everything he ever told her had been a lie to entice her into bed. Breaking it off, she fooled herself into believing she could continue to work at his company as usual. After all, she had a monumental responsibility.

Ensuring that her brother recovered from his numerous injuries, walked again, and had the wonderful life her beloved parents envisioned for him came before all else in Amara's life. Amara just didn't want her fabulous salary and commissions; she needed them. But Terrence wanted what he wanted. He claimed he'd been working on a divorce because he had to be with Amara. Denying him her affection, she tried to be just friends. Terrence found that unacceptable and acted spitefully. Every second of her workday, he made difficult. If he didn't criticize Amara's handling of clients, he found fault with her for a thousand trivial matters.

Then, one evening when the two of them had worked late in the office, Terrence tried to make love to her. When Amara rejected him, he flew into a rage and fired her. He threatened he would write up the reason as incompetence with her responsibilities. On the other hand, if she had a change of heart, the job was hers again.

The following day, Amara consulted an attorney. A half hour later, she walked out of his office disheartened. She had dated Terrence. Her co-workers knew of it. If she filed a sexual harassment lawsuit and lost the case, she might have to pay for all attorneys' fees, even for a countersuit. How could she afford such a defeat when her brother had costly medical care? Hence, she pounded the pavement for another position.

Amara landed another job in her profession. Shortly after, an unknown and larger company bought out the real estate firm within a few weeks of her employment. The new owner already had his own agents in place to make the transition. Oddly, the same thing happened with the second company that hired her.

Soon after, Amara learned from a former coworker at Terrence's firm that he had purchased all of the leading realty companies in the area. Continuously, Amara questioned whether the acquisitions were simply about business. Or had he attempted to make her life hell out of spite? After all, when each company sent for references, Terrence had to verify her employment dates. So he knew where she worked at all times.

Thereafter, Amara became acquainted with the unemployment problem that beset the rest of the country. During this time the months swept by. Her extensive savings dwindled, while her bills added up. The largest expense turned out to be the cost of her brother's rehabilitation. After Derrick's near fatal skiing accident, two years ago while he was on his college's winter break, insurance covered a major portion of his medical costs. Amara covered the rest, which were running out of her pocket substantially.

The first two rehabilitation centers appeared to make Derrick worse instead of better. Equally disheartening, each facility gave a bleak prognosis. It wasn't until she began dating Terrence did she become aware of The Holoman Therapy Center. Located two towns away from her home, it had a reputation for being one of the finest facilities in the country to assist those suffering with head and spinal injuries.

Terrence's cousin had recuperated there and been rehabilitated after an accident which had caused partial paralysis. He had raved about the center. The steep price didn't deter Amara from Derrick's transfer there. It proved to be a fantastic move. His condition improved immediately. What's more, Terrence raised Amara's salary and commission rate substantially, so she could afford the steep cost of her brother's treatments. But now stripped of her cushy income, she feared for her brother's fate. Losing the other two jobs added to a feeling of hopelessness.

But the pity party didn't last long. After shaking off her worry, Amara refused to let anything disrupt her brother's progress. She sold valuable heirlooms, which broke her heart to part with. She even sold one of her two cars, her BMW, and drove her clunker. She took any employment opportunity offered her. Her savings had dwindled to zero when she spotted the advertisement for a high salaried nude artist's model in a college campus newspaper.

Now, she sprawled in a luxurious bed in a mansion. The night had certainly taken her on an adventure. As horrible as her car conking out and losing her home appeared to be, a sweet surprise had come her way: Bryce Davidson.

After wolfing down a near box full of Famous Amos Chocolate Chip Cookies in the kitchen, Bryce's long, muscled legs climbed his lengthy staircase. He headed to his bedroom thinking about something that he shouldn't have. But how could he force his brain to stop thinking and seeing what obsessed him? And how could he make his body stop desiring what nearly drove him mad all night? When he reached the second floor, the telephone rang from where it set on an antique, console table.

Bryce swiped up the cordless receiver. "Hello?"

"What's up, my brother?" Terrence asked in an exuberant voice. "What's up? What's up? What's up?"

Bryce tuned out from his buddy. Not only did he feel uneasy because he was thinking about Amara in ways that he shouldn't have, but he was also wondering if he should tell him that he invited her to spend the night in his home.

"Hey?" Terrence called. "You're still there?"

"Yes, I'm here."

"Guess what happened tonight?"

"What?" Bryce sensed something exciting had his partner's spirits high.

"Oh, just that I came from dinner with Swanson and we closed the deal on the Porter Condominiums."

"Yes!" Bryce raised his fist in victory. Numerous real estate investors had tried to purchase the property. It was not only a lucrative piece of real estate, but also one that would enable Bryce to do community and charitable projects.

"I'll go over the paperwork with you tomorrow, but we came out real nice, bro. Real nice."

"That's great, man." He glanced down the hall at the bedroom where Amara slept. "I'm happy about that."

"I'm happy, too. If it wasn't for you partnering with me, I wouldn't have been able to make all this crazy stuff happen. I can't thank you enough."

"I'm glad…I'm glad to help." Bryce faded away, still debating if he should mention Amara. If his ex-girlfriend had been in the same situation with Terrence, what would he have wanted him to do? Yet he knew dwelling on it all was foolish. They had been best friends since playing on the basketball team in high school. Now, this year, both of them turned thirty-nine.

"Are you okay?" Terrence's voice pulled him from his thoughts. "What did you do tonight? Get a piece that turned you out?" He let out a quick, wild laugh.

Bryce's full mouth curved in a devilish grin. "No, it's nothing like that."

"Then what? Sounds like something is bothering you."

"Nothing is really bothering me. It's just that I need to tell you something."

"What?"

"It's Amara."

"Amara?" Terrence echoed dramatically. "What about Amara? You heard about something happening to her?"

"No, nothing happened to her. It's just that she's here."

"She's there! What the hell is she doing at your place?"

"She's staying in one of my spare rooms tonight because she had no place to go."

"What? No place to go?"

Bryce explained that it surprised him to see Amara modeling in his art class. Sidestepping the subject of her nudity, he went further into details, recounting the events that followed. "I hope you don't mind that she's here," he said, glancing down the hall again. "I just didn't know what else to do. I couldn't leave a woman in the street like that."

"No, you couldn't," Terrence agreed, "but why didn't you call me?"

"You? Man, you forget you confided in me about Amara. I know how pissed you were at the woman."

"And I remember how pissed you were at me, too, for not telling her about Michelle."

"Look, let's not get into that again. I don't know what it's

17

like to want to end it with your wife and then she goes into a mental institution. So I shouldn't be judging."

"The marriage was over long before she went away," Terrence replied coldly

"You've told me that over and over."

"So don't judge me!" Terrence snapped.

Bryce reared back from the sharp tone in his friend's voice. "Man, I said I'm not."

"But you wouldn't have done it, would you?"

"Done what?" Bryce asked.

"Been with someone else while your wife was in the loony bin, even if you were on the verge of divorcing her before she lost her mind?"

"Come on, man. Why don't we talk about the deal?"

"Why don't you answer my question? I promise I won't get mad," Terrence replied calmly.

Bryce thought for a moment. He disagreed with the way Terrence treated Michelle, but he had always held his tongue. He simply disliked interfering in other's relationships, especially his best friend. "All right, no," Bryce admitted finally. "I wouldn't have done it."

"I know you wouldn't have," Terrence said. "But you've done something I couldn't have done either. To this day, I still don't know how you did it."

Bryce's breath flowed over the receiver as he thought back to another time. "It felt right at the time."

"Huh," Terrence remarked. "If you say so. Anyway, I'm coming to see Amara tomorrow."

"That's not a good idea."

"What do you mean it's not a good idea? Who are you to tell me what to do?"

"I mean, I don't want any mess coming down in my house, Tee. I brought this woman here to help her, not for you to come over here and make her feel worse than she already does."

"Do you think I would really do that?" Terrence asked.

"To be honest, I don't know. You were pretty pissed at her one time ago."

Terrence chuckled dryly. "Oh, I don't feel that way now. I miss her. I want to see her. I want to talk to her. I want to help, and I'm coming tomorrow." Terrence added with a sly tone, "I bet she looks good."

Bryce had no comment. No way could he express how good Amara looked—how good every naked inch of her body looked. Just the mental image of her in the class made his heart race. "All right, come. Just no mess, please."

"There won't be any. Now, I'm going to get some sleep. You get some, too."

Bryce hung up the phone and gazed down the hall. He questioned his judgment for giving in to Terrence. Terrence felt like his brother in every sense of the word. Throughout the years, they had shared each other's triumphs, as well as tribulations. Terrence would do anything for him and vice versa. Being as it may, he had witnessed his best friend do twisted things when it came to getting what he desired from a woman.

Deciding he needed to let Amara know about Terrence's visit tomorrow, Bryce strolled toward the guestroom. He knocked. She didn't answer. He walked away. Feelings slowed him, the ones that came alive in him the moment he walked into the classroom and saw her beautiful face and equally beautiful body. Visualizing her that way again, he couldn't help himself. Bryce walked back and cracked the bedroom door to look in.

Dim light shaded the room from a night table lamp left on. Sleeping with her lips softly parted, Amara's face belonged in a fantasy. Her long, cinnamon-hued mane scattered wildly over the pillow, framing her exotic features like a halo. Her satin-skinned body flattened on the silken, blue sheets with parts of her shapely legs exposed from the lacey bedspread. She appeared to be naked beneath the covers, with the most arousing part for him exposed, a naked breast protruded skyward. The nipple looked like a ripe berry ready for a kiss.

Feeling a super erection, like the one when he first saw Amara naked in class, Bryce couldn't budge until he saw her squirming as if she might wake. No way would he let her catch him ogling her like a pervert. He had been raised to be a gentleman. Promptly he closed

19

the door. His Nikes thumped along the russet hardwood floor en
route to the hallway bathroom. The bathroom in his bedroom, as well
as the remainder of the bathrooms in the bedrooms, were currently
undergoing renovations and unavailable.

Hastily, Bryce tossed his clothes on the floor. The room had
pale green walls and matching marble floor. He eyed the Jacuzzi and the
shower. Choosing the latter, he grabbed a coconut-scented soap and
stepped inside. A mixture of hot and cold water pelted him. Groaning,
red heat surging through him, he grabbed his huge penis. He shut his
eyes tight and reared his head back.

With the warm stream sluicing him, he imagined tasting
Amara's plump lips until his tongue eased in her mouth and made love
with hers greedily. He imagined his fingers exploring all over her flesh
and playing deep within her, making her whimper for him to give her
his love. He imagined burying his head between her trembling thighs,
inhaling her scent, and lapping her sweet pearl, making her so wet
that she shook and screamed from the unbearable pleasure. Mostly,
he imagined staring into Amara's eyes as he opened her legs wide, and
placed his long, black penis inside her tight juiciness, and moved to an
addictive rhythm that made them come hard, as if they never came
before. Yes, Bryce imagined and imagined. But it wasn't the first time
sexual fantasies about Amara possessed him.

When he first left Chicago and partnered with Terrence, his
buddy wasted no time in letting him know which agent in the office
had been his lover. Because Amara called off their affair, Terrence had
been furious and he had verbally ripped her apart. His sharp tongue
did nothing to diminish her in Bryce's eyes.

Amara's sexy looks not only got under his skin, but so did
her warm and genuine personality. In some strange way, he knew her.
While in reality, they worked together for merely three weeks before
her termination. In the days leading up to it, whenever Terrence talked
to Bryce in private, he belittled Amara, furnishing details about what
she was like in bed. If only Terrence knew he had picked the wrong
man to confide with. Foul as Bryce knew Terrence's comments were,
he couldn't stop thinking about Amara.

After Terrence forced her out of the company, Bryce often

wondered about her. Nevertheless, he realized the distance served him well. If out of sight long enough, Amara would eventually be out of mind. Some other sultry creature would come along and quench his fascination with her. They had no future anyway. In no way would he betray Terrence, just as Terrence wouldn't betray him. Dating his best friend and business partner's ex-lover was something he just didn't do.

Walking into the art class and seeing Amara was the best surprise life had given him in a long time. As she shed her robe, his eyes had the great fortune to feast on her in all her delicious glory. Bryce felt turned on in ways he never knew possible. Seeing her like that was like a dream.

Stripped of every piece of clothing, Amara looked sexier than she had in the sensual shows that invaded his mind. As he sketched her portrait, thoughts of what he could do with all that luscious, forbidden fruit distracted him. Repeatedly Bryce shook his legs to calm himself because he felt hard enough to explode. He couldn't stop fantasizing he was alone with Amara in class, kissing every inch of her, inside and out.

Bryce stepped out of the shower onto the cool marble. Swiping up a large, brown towel hanging on the side of the Jacuzzi, he glimpsed himself in the mirror. Turning his face from side to side, he admitted he needed to shave. He admitted something else too, all these thoughts of making love with Amara should go no further.

Regardless of how irrationally Terrence behaved, Bryce knew Terrence had loved her. Probably still did. So what kind of friend would he be if he acted on something, acted on the vibe he sensed from Amara tonight? Did his mind play tricks on him? Or did she really look as if she wanted to feel his lips against hers?

The questions lingered as Bryce wrapped the knee-length towel around his narrow hips. He flipped off the light switch, stepped into the hall, and nearly collided with Amara.

"Oh!" Amara jumped back, grabbing her chest. "You scared me."

"Sorry about that." Bryce's dark eyes smiled at her and he noticed she had covered her curves in the white kimono she'd worn in art class. He assumed she was naked beneath it. "I would never want to scare you."

To his reply, Amara laughed softly and stared at his bare chest and then at the towel.

"I uh…I needed to go to the bathroom," she stammered. "I saw that the one in the bedroom is having work done. I remembered seeing this one in the hall," she quickly added.

"I forgot to tell you about the renovations." Looking down, he tucked in his towel more securely. The growing bulge beneath slackened it. If he didn't get away from Amara soon, he would be embarrassed. "I'm sorry."

"It's okay."

When Bryce finally looked up, he caught Amara's eyes locked on his towel. His erection formed a huge tent with it, but the hunger in her face didn't make him feel embarrassed, at all. In fact, he wanted her to look. Even better, he wanted her to touch him.

Their gazes eventually met and a strained silence preceded him asking in a husky whisper, "Is there anything you want or need?"

Chapter Three

Amara fought the moist pulses between her legs as she stood in front of Bryce. If he could have felt the wild thumping in her chest, he wouldn't have to ask his question. The way Bryce looked, the way he looked at her, the way he smelled, and the way she obviously stimulated him, turned her on. If she had any doubts about his attraction to her, she didn't have them now. Just a few inches closer and she could have felt his hardness. Just a tug of his towel and Amara knew she would have beheld so much man that she would need him deep inside of her.

Having sex with a man she hardly knew was something she'd never done before. She even refused to have sex with a man she wasn't in love with. It was just her nature. Still, Bryce tempted her. With all of the special equipment he had obviously been blessed with, God knows he could have surely eased her pain.

Not since Terrence had made love to her on his mansion's terrace had she been with a man. Now, here she stood desiring to recreate another hot scene with not only Terrence's business partner, but best friend. She couldn't come between them. More importantly, she couldn't put her heart out there again. She wouldn't allow another man to break it.

"I don't want anything," Amara answered hesitantly. "Just need to use the little girl's room. But thanks for asking."

Bryce nodded slowly. "All right. You get a good night's sleep."

"You, too," she quietly replied and shyly turned away from Bryce.

Bryce stepped around her. Soon, she was alone, wondering

what could have been.

"It's the fuel pump," a sandy-haired fellow with skin the hue of a biscuit informed Bryce. Well after sunrise the next morning, Sampson "Red" Jones rested his chubby hand on Amara's car trunk. The two men stood on the oily concrete in Red's Auto Body Shop.

Bryce expelled a relieved breath. Amara's car wasn't beyond repair. Fortunately, he had forgotten to return her keys after his attempt to start up her engine in the parking lot. After the ordeal she experienced, he wanted to surprise her and lift her spirits. Before dawn, he phoned his mechanic and had the car towed to the shop to be repaired.

He couldn't bear the thought of Amara fretting about how to get to work or visit her brother. And if Terrence didn't approve of him helping her out, tough for him. His buddy had told him plenty about the steamy affair, and Amara breaking it off rocked Terrence's world.

Still, Bryce couldn't understand why his friend was so spiteful. Why did he have to fire Amara, especially in light of her brother's situation? Obviously, the pink slip led to her financial ruin. What's more, it made no sense from a business perspective. Amara was one of TJ Realty's top-selling agents. Bryce shook his head at Terrence's thinking.

"Red," Bryce addressed his mechanic.

Red wiped his soiled hands on a rag. "Yeah, what's the word, man?"

"Give the car a new fuel pump and whatever else it may need."

Amara had wakened, showered, and dressed in a yellow, cotton skirt set and bone colored medium-heeled mules when she left the bedroom at mid-morning. Calling to Bryce as her shoes clacked against the stairs, she wished she hadn't slept in so late. But the bed had felt heavenly once her mind had relaxed enough to let her doze off. When she wasn't worrying about her situation, she was wondering about Bryce.

Downstairs, Amara searched the living room, peeked in Bryce's home office, poked her head in the kitchen, and then stepped outside. Inhaling a nearby rosebush's scent, she entered the garage where her belongings were. While she gathered a handful of toiletries stashed among her things, she hoped to see Bryce soon. She wanted to tell him what she had decided to do about her dilemma.

After leaving the garage, Amara noticed a black Jaguar driving on the estate's S shaped road. Her heart stuttered. Terrence owned a car of a similar model and color. As the sedan coasted nearer, she drew a breath. The bright sunshine caused her to squint, accentuating how incensed she appeared about Terrence's unwanted visit. Why had Bryce invited him there?

Dimples pinched Terrence's cheeks as he slammed the car's door. His tall, athletic form, decked out in a dark blue tailored suit, walked her way. "You look good, baby. Real good," he crooned, attempting to hug her.

Amara moved back, avoiding contact. "Why are you here, Terrence?"

"Isn't it obvious? I miss you," he said, looking boyish and sincere.

Amara rolled her eyes and the rage from all that he had done to her felt like it gathered in a knot in her chest.

"I do miss you."

She shook her head and tried to settle her fiercely pounding heart. "I can't believe Bryce did this to me! I can't believe it!"

"Did this to you?" Terrence's gold-brown eyes grew steely, despite his smile. "You're acting like I'm the plague or something. Baby, I came to help you. Help you like I did with your brother. How is he by the way?"

Amara glared at him. He had some nerve to act as if he cared about her brother after all he had done to hurt her. "He's still at the therapy center," she responded after several seconds, "but he's getting better."

"That's beautiful. It's like a miracle, isn't it? A miracle I made

Kiss Me All Over

happen," Terrence said with a look of satisfaction.

"And you'll never let me forget either."

"I'm really hurt. Any other woman would be appreciative."

"I am appreciative. It was a very nice thing you did for Derrick and me. Very nice." She brushed a long lock of hair away from her face. "But constantly reminding me of what you did isn't nice. And you know what else is pretty darn nasty, causing my unemployment."

A scowl suddenly distorted his smooth, bronzed face. "You can't put it on me if you're in a tight spot."

"Why can't I? You not only fired me because I wouldn't continue sleeping with you, but you bought up the companies I worked for, forcing me out of two additional jobs."

"You worked for Henderson and Wentworth?" he asked with a slight grin on his face.

Her mink-hued eyes rolled heavenward at his innocent act. "You know I did."

"No, really, I had no idea you worked at either of them."

"You did know. You bought them because you wanted me to be out of a job and fall flat on my face. But you know, I'm still standing." Her lips curled in a grin.

Terrence smirked. "But not too well from what I hear, baby. Believe me, I simply made a business decision."

"Yeah, you were in the business of ruining my life because I didn't want you!"

"That's not true. To prove it, I'm asking you to come back to TJ Realty, to your former position. You were a great asset to the company, one of my top agents. In fact, the company sales are so astronomical right now I can give you a substantial increase in salary and commission rate." He smiled gently. "What do you say?"

"And I get hassled each day because I won't get in your bed." She folded her arms. "How is your wife by the way?"

Terrence glanced aside as if had to think about the answer. "She's the same, but I'm still going to divorce her."

"Why are you telling me that?"

"Because…" He searched her face heatedly. "I want you, baby. I still want you."

26

"If I came back, you would sexually harass me."

He shook his head. "No, I wouldn't do that. I want you to come back because you're a helluva real estate agent. However, if you did want to be with me, I can't lie. I would be happy about that. But there wouldn't be any pressure, I promise. So think about it."

Amara considered his proposal, even though she felt foolish doing so. She had less than a hundred dollars in her purse, no savings account to speak of, no apartment, and a brother whose medical bills were so whopping they sometimes gave her migraines. She couldn't help but think about his offer, regardless of her feelings for Terrence. On the other hand, she knew how much trouble Terrence was, and she was no fool.

"So where are you going to stay after you leave here today?" He looked up at Bryce's mansion, and then shifted his attention to her. "I can help you out, you know. It's not a problem."

"No thanks. I'm going to stay with a friend."

"And what about this modeling?"

She braced herself for what Bryce obviously told him. "What about it?"

"What are you posing in gowns or something?"

She hid her relief. At least Bryce hadn't blabbed about her posing in the nude. "Why do you care, Terrence?"

"Because I do." He reached to touch her, but her irate expression backed him off. "You don't have to model in some class. You're a top real estate agent with a position waiting for you. And Bryce would agree with me. Where is my man, anyway?"

"I have no idea. When I woke up, he was nowhere around. I guess he's gone out."

"Probably out jogging or chasing a beautiful woman just like I am." He chuckled, and then glimpsed his watch. "Well, I have a meeting and have to get going. But I want you to think about the offer and get in touch with me."

When Bryce returned home, he headed straight to the guest room. It was empty. The bed looked tidy and traces of a woman's perfume lingered in the air. He smiled, remembering how it smelled on Amara when they stood near each other. Looking for her in the other rooms throughout the mansion, Bryce called out to her. By the time he stood in the garage where her belongings were, he scratched his head with bafflement. Would it have been that hard to scribble him a note? He just wanted to know if she was going to be all right.

Taking a seat on one of Amara's boxes, Bryce wondered if their close encounter in the bathroom last night offended her. Had he made Amara uncomfortable? And was she too nice to not call him a dog for him having the erection of all erections?

He hadn't meant to come off like a horny hound ready to jump her bones. It was just that she affected him, really affected him. And he knew Amara felt it as much as he did. Moreover, he knew she wanted something to happen. Her eyes didn't lie.

Pulling himself to his feet, other thoughts came to mind. He had been so busy getting her car repaired he had almost forgotten Terrence was supposed to drop by. Had the fire they once shared reignited? Had Amara run off with him? Or had Terrence acted like a jackass and frightened her away?

Bryce hoped neither was the case. He was anxious to deliver the good news about her car. Hopefully he could do that later.

Bryce smiled, remembering his evening class with Amara. Once again, he could enjoy the sight of her completely naked. Just thinking about it, he closed his eyes and moaned.

The tiny window in the University's changing room allowed the early evening sun to light the room. Captivated by the breathtaking view, Amara snapped herself out of the trance and lowered her gaze to do what she had loathed to do, get undressed. As she disrobed, it killed her she had to resort to such drastic measures to earn a living. Not that nude modeling, for the sake of art was degrading, because it wasn't. It just wasn't her dream.

Amara's folded garments set on a chair as she pulled a pink, silk cover up from a tote bag. Slipping her toned arms into the delicate fabric, jitters about baring it all to strangers tormented her just as it had the previous evening. Though, one of the students was not a stranger. That student had entertained her with an unforgettable night.

After their brush at the bathroom, Amara had been tempted to go to Bryce's bedroom. She longed to discover what he had beneath his towel and how well he knew how to use it. The desire wasn't purely about lust, but about making her pain go away. One look in Bryce's eyes guaranteed he could have accomplished that task.

Yet this morning, she learned he had deceived her. Apparently, Bryce couldn't wait to call Terrence to prattle about how far she had fallen without him. She surmised Bryce likely had tooted his horn about rescuing her from the streets. Amara imagined the twosome probably wagered how long it would take before she came crawling back to TJ Realty, to Terrence, and to his bed.

As she entered the class, Amara hoped Bryce had skipped tonight's session. A glimpse at the sea of faces showed no such luck. Seated in the front row, Bryce appeared as if he were holding his breath waiting for her to take off her kimono. The professor lectured about artistic techniques for a half-hour. At that point, he asked Amara to model.

Looking down instead of at the class, she loosened the sash and posed in a sensuous, but tasteful manner on the table. Once she diverted her attention from the aspiring artists, her eyes instantly found Bryce, as if he was the only person in the classroom. A subtle smile curled his broad mouth as their gazes met. Amara didn't return the pleasant expression. Her slanted eyes narrowed and she looked away.

The class was quiet as the students sat at their easels and made strokes across their canvases. To get through the moments, Amara tried to fantasize she was somewhere else, somewhere more pleasurable than on this table with Bryce watching her so intently. It was useless. She couldn't resist glancing to where Bryce sat.

Each time Amara looked at him, he studied her body and then studied her eyes. Several times, she swore she saw tenderness in his gaze. Knowing he was Terrence's best friend, and shown himself to be just like him, she attributed his gaze to pure male lust.

The second class ended, Amara grasped her kimono. While tying the belt, she heard the frail-looking instructor commanding everyone's attention.

"Sadly, I must tell you all that this will be the last evening of our class."

Amara drew a breath, while disappointed utterances swirled around her.

The professor raised his vein-streaked hands to quiet everyone. "You will all be refunded the remainder of your fee for the class. The reason for the course ending is that I received a job offer to head the art department at a Parisian university. And I couldn't turn it down. It's a life-changing opportunity. I'm so sorry. They are interviewing for a new instructor, but at present, one isn't available with the high standards this university requires. You will be notified when a new instructor is found."

The students surrounded the professor, wishing him well and grilling him about various matters concerning the defunct class. Devastated at her rotten luck, Amara stood motionless, contemplating her next move. Until, that is, she saw Bryce approaching her. Before he reached her, she walked out of the room.

After putting on her clothes, Amara hurried into the university parking lot. She planned to try to start up her wheels once more. If unsuccessful, she intended to explain her plight to security. They could advise her on their policy. She guessed they would call for a tow. Whenever she had the funds, she would reclaim her property.

Stepping briskly toward the area where she left the car, Amara saw Bryce waiting in her path. He appeared thrilled as she came his way. Pissed at him, she couldn't even force a smile. Nevertheless, when they faced each other, his dark, luminous eyes gazed at her so warmly she almost forgot her disappointment in him.

"Your friend paid me a visit this morning while you were out," she informed him.

Bryce dabbed his mustache. "I meant to--."

"Why did you have to tell Terrence about me? Did you want him to know I had fallen so low?"

Bryce frowned. "No, not at all. I--"

"Did you get a kick out of telling him you're such a big man you had to rescue me? Otherwise, I would be out on the streets?"

30

"He called last night and it didn't seem right not to tell him you were at my house. I know you two ended badly, but you were in a relationship, and he is my friend. Look, I'm sorry you feel the way you do. My parents raised me to be a gentleman, and treat people the way I would like to be treated. That's all I was trying to do." His frown deepening, he pulled her car keys out of his jeans' pocket and handed them to her.

Amara's brown eyes widened. "I forgot you had my keys."

"Yes you did. And your car is not this way. It's over there." He pointed across the lot.

Amara peered in the direction. Her old red jalopy shined, as it never had before. Stunned, she gazed back at Bryce. "It had a paint job?"

"The car had everything it needed." His tone was firm. "The major problem was the fuel pump. My mechanic drove it back. That's why it's not in the original spot."

"Oh, my goodness." She clutched her chest and tried to settle her racing heart. "I really, really appreciate this."

"Well, you're set now. Take care."

Bryce strode off with sadness in his gait, which multiplied the guilt she suddenly felt.

"Bryce?" Her heels clacked against the concrete as she ran to catch up with him.

He turned around as she reached him. "Yes?"

"I'm sorry I went off on you. You're the last person I should have done that to. You let me stay in your home, put my things in your garage, fixed my car. You didn't have to do any of those things. For someone I hardly know, you sure did a lot for me."

"It's all right, Amara."

"No, it's not. What I said to you wasn't right. I guess all the problems I've had doesn't make me think straight. They make me think the worst about everything, especially people. You just don't know the things I've been through."

His scowl relaxed and his dusky eyes searched her face gently. "Maybe you can tell me about it all one day...I mean if you just want to talk."

31

"I might take you up on that." Smiling, she had a flash of him in that towel again. Lord knows, what she would have seen if he had yanked the towel off.

As if a naughty thought crossed his mind as well, Amara noticed Bryce sneaking looks at her body. "So uh…are you coming back to my house?"

"No, I'm going to stay with my friend, Jamie. But if you don't mind, I'd like to leave everything in your garage, except for my clothes. I'll take those for now."

"You don't have to take anything. You're welcome to stay at my place."

"That's very nice of you, but no." She knew Terrence would have flipped out.

Nodding, his eyes still slinked along her figure. "All right. Then at least let me help you with job prospects. What about coming back to TJ?"

"Actually Terrence asked me to work there again, but I'm not accepting it."

"I can understand that." He peered off thinking, and then focused on her again. "There could be another position available in light of the art class ending tonight."

"And what is that?" She grew excited from just the look on his face.

His gaze reached deep in hers and his voice dwindled to a near whisper. He asked, "How about being my private model? I would still like to draw and paint you."

Chapter Four

"Pose for you privately?" Amara questioned with widened eyes.

"Forget it." Bryce regretted making such a proposition the instant the words slipped past his lips. Amara's shocked look told him he should have kept his secret desire in check. The thought of Terrence and how he would react crossed his mind. "I was out of line."

"It's okay," she said, intrigued and titillated by the offer.

"No, Amara, it wasn't cool, and I apologize."

"You just wanted to help me."

"That I do."

They skirted around the uncomfortable moment with talk about possible job prospects. Minutes later, Amara's refurbished wheels trailed Bryce's back to his home. She planned to haul her clothes and other items to Jamie's place.

At Bryce's estate, Amara and he carried her clothing from the garage to her car. Taking note of the huge amount of outfits and accessories she owned, he couldn't resist teasing her. "What do you do with all of these clothes?" He bent down into the backseat of her car and placed several pairs of slacks along the cushions. When he stood and faced Amara, she looked playful and mischievousness.

"I style and profile, that's what I do."

"Is that right?"

"Of course." She tossed some handbags in the front seat and strolled back to the garage for more items.

Bryce trailed her. "I like to style and profile, too, right in my dingy jeans and sweats, over and over."

Amara chuckled. "What about those nice suits you have?"

"What nice suits?"

"The ones you wore when I worked at TJ. You never wore the same suit twice. They were all either tailored or Italian cut, and fitted your body like a glove."

Bryce smiled with surprise. Amara had actually noticed his wardrobe, and his body. "I have to wear those for work."

"Well your admirers appreciated it."

"My admirers?" he echoed as they entered the garage again.

"Yep." She scanned the crowded area for more of her things. "There were plenty of them when I worked there."

Intrigued by her statement, Bryce took a seat on a large box. "And who might they be?"

"The women at TJ."

"Which ones?"

Her eyes locked with his and she flashed a saucy grin. "Certainly you can tell."

"I don't have a clue."

"Really? Because I always thought a man knows when a woman is interested, just like a woman does."

Absorbing the words, Bryce watched her. Amara returned his gaze steadily and looked like she wanted to share something more. But after awhile, she focused back on locating her belongings. Bryce stood, knowing he treaded dangerously close to doing or saying something which he shouldn't have. He picked up the box he had sat upon and walked out of the garage. After he placed it in the trunk, Amara caught up to him. She set several boxes of shoes in the trunk.

With his handkerchief, he wiped sweat from his forehead and studied her again. The dusk had turned her skin an orange-brown, and because of her constant movement, a light sheen of perspiration dusted her face, arms, chest, legs.

"So what about TJ?" he asked.

"What about it?"

"Will you at least think about coming back? As I said before, I understand your hesitation. Terrence acted the fool, but people can change. Maybe he is trying to make up for it."

"How can he make up for putting me through hell? You just don't know what he did to me. But then again, maybe you do. I'm sure

34

he told you everything."

"Forget what he told me. If you ever want to tell me anything, I'm here. And I will keep it between us."

Her full lips formed a soft smile. "I appreciate that. And again, I appreciate you letting me stay at your lovely home and fixing my car. I will repay you."

"I'm not concerned about repayment. I just wish you could stay longer. When the weather is nice like this, I like to grill up some lobster and shrimp, and make some of the best salad you ever tasted. But it's no fun just grilling for myself."

"Oh, I'll be back. I can't fit all of my clothes in this car."

"You can use my van."

"Nope, I have an excuse to come back."

"Oh, so you do want to see me again. I didn't scare you off, after all?"

"How could you possibly scare me off?"

"You never know," he answered, as a flash of them at the bathroom entrance came to mind. He shook it off, and further shook off the impulse to ask her to pose for him privately again. He had to be a gentleman. It didn't matter that every second he spent around this woman, he wanted her more and more.

Cruising down the darkening highway, Amara twisted the radio dial. The mechanic, who had left whiffs of auto oil in her car and repaired its problems, had clearly switched the radio station. The knob had moved from her R&B oldies station to a top 40 one. When she heard Marvin Gaye croon "What's Going On", her head swayed until thoughts of Bryce filtered through the soulful sounds.

Why did he keep looking at her that way? What possessed him to ask her to pose for a private portrait? Was it the same thing, which tempted her to say yes? Would he have merely behaved as an artist and tried to paint her in her bare flesh? Or would he have kissed off his friendship with Terrence and dared to entice her into a more risqué act? God knows the imagery of stripping before him and seeing what happened next didn't seem quite as discomforting as it did before. In fact, it titillated and excited her just as much as the sight of him in that towel did.

Twenty minutes later Amara steered her car into the driveway of Jamie's brick row house. They had become friends while Jamie worked at TJ Realty. However, Jamie's dream to become an airline stewardess led her to resign from her position. Amara remained close with her girlfriend. When she called Jamie this morning and shared her dilemma, Amara didn't get a chance to ask for an enormous favor. Jamie offered Amara a room, immediately.

After stepping up a short flight of stairs, Amara rang the doorbell. She was enjoying the perfume from a nearby potpourri of flowers tucked in the shadows when the door swung open. A vibrant smile that didn't match the harsh, hazel eyes, faced her. Jamie's cousin, Carlyn, a slender beauty with a wild, black afro, also lived at the house. Amara knew her because she too had once worked for TJ Realty, but had been laid off when the company downsized.

"What's up?" Carlyn greeted her, as she leaned in the door frame.

Amara granted her a warm smile. "I'm all right. How are you?"

"Great. Just got a promotion at the hotel I work at. I'm a manager now."

"Jamie told me. That's wonderful. Congratulations."

"So what are you doing now that you're not working for Terrence? You're an agent somewhere else?"

"No, actually, I'm looking for work right now."

"Wow, that's too bad. Maybe Terrence can help. Do you still see each other?"

Amara kept a pleasant face, despite Carlyn's unwanted prying. Though, she understood why Jamie's cousin behaved this way, Carlyn used to flirt with Terrence. While they worked together at TJ, it was obvious she wanted their boss. He didn't reciprocate the attraction.

"Oh, I don't want to bore you with the details about Terrence and me," Amara answered. "I'm sure you have so many interesting things going on in your life you could care less about us."

Carlyn looked like she wanted to respond, but didn't know

how to. As she looked confused with her lips moving with no sound coming out, Amara heard heavy footsteps approach the front door. Once Jamie's petite body came into view, Amara wondered how such a small person could make such a big sound?

Stepping into the doorway, Jaime frowned at Carlyn. "Girl, why do you have her standing out here?"

Carlyn opened the door further for Amara to enter. "I forgot she was staying."

Overlooking Carlyn's games, Amara walked inside the house and hugged Jamie. Due to Jamie's hectic flight schedule and Amara's job hunt, they hadn't seen each other in a few months. After their affectionate greeting, Amara caught Jamie up on the day's interesting events. They continued their girl talk in the bedroom Jamie offered Amara.

"My clothes are in the car," Amara said, kicking back on a beige chaise. "I'll get them out in the morning. I'm too pooped to bother now."

On the bed, Jamie curled her plump legs to one side. "That's fine. Just stay there and relax. But girl, you have to tell me more about your time with Prince Charming."

"Who is that?"

"Bryce, of course."

Amara suddenly glowed. "What more do you want to know? I told you the man was wonderful to me. He let me stay at his place and leave my things there."

"And he fixed your car."

"Yes, that too."

"So you know he wouldn't do all that for just anyone."

"He's a gentleman. He might."

Jamie just looked at her. "Come on now, he's a man."

"That's hard to miss."

"He's a man who is interested."

Amara eyed her curiously. "What are you talking about?"

"I'm talking about what I picked up on when I worked with you both. Even though he was Terrence's friend and a nice guy, I got the impression he was interested in you."

"You never told me this."

"Girl, did I sign a legal agreement that I have to tell you everything in my brain?"

Amara let out a gentle laugh. "Well, you should have told me. What made you feel this way? Did he say something to you, or someone else?"

"No, nothing was said. It was just how he interacted with you in the office. I also saw him staring a lot on the sly. Nothing gets past these big ones." Jamie stretched her big, brown eyes.

Amara laughed again. "You're crazy. But it is interesting what you noticed."

"What do you mean? What happened?" Jamie uncurled her legs and shifted to the bottom of the bed. The chaise Amara rested on set near the bed. "Did something happen at his place?"

Amara kidded her with silence and gave her friend a naughty look.

"What?" Jamie hopped to her feet. "Girl, you had some of that delicious looking man? Whooh, child, please tell me what it was like?"

"No," Amara said immediately and her face flushed. "But I did see him half naked."

"What!"

Amara went on to recount the incident at the bathroom, and later repeated his question to pose for him privately. At the windup, Jamie shook her head full of short curls.

"Girl, he wants to tear it up. The truth literally stood up for you."

Amara burst into laughter. "You're crazy like I said. Crazy, crazy, crazy."

"Why don't you just let him help himself?"

"No, you're just plain freaky, Jamie Owens."

"Freaky my foot. You haven't had any since what century?"

Amara tossed a throw pillow at her.

Jamie caught it and laughed, then sobered. "No, but really I'm serious. Bryce is attracted to you. And if I'm reading you right --that look in your eyes, and that big, goofy grin you have now--it all says you're attracted to him, too."

Amara blushed. "He's fine as can be. He's real sweet, too. But he's Terrence's best friend and business partner. I can't get into that."

"Why not? Terrence and you are over."

"Yes, but he and Terrence aren't over. They are in business and I just don't want to get between two friends."

"You don't have to throw it in his face."

"No, it's not a good idea. Besides, I'm not ready. I'm not ready for an involvement with anyone after what Terrence did to me. Plus, I haven't spent that much time around Bryce to know if this sweet side of him is genuine. He is Terrence's friend. Given some time, he may be just like him. Terrence was sweet in the beginning, too."

"I don't know. I think you might be missing out."

"And I may be missing on more than Bryce, too. When I saw Terrence today, he offered me a job at TJ Realty with a substantial increase in salary and commission."

"What did you say?"

"No, of course. I want nothing to do with that man."

"But what are you going to do about money since your job ended today?"

"Are you encouraging me to take it? You know what Terrence put me through."

"Hey, I can't tell you what to do. And you're welcome to stay here as long as you want, free room and board. But what about Derrick? How are you going to pay for his medical care with no income?"

The next morning Amara showered, ate, dressed and left the house early. Destined for the Holomon Therapy Center to see her brother, she drove down the highway with the windows rolled down, taking in the purplish dawn and inhaling fresh morning air. God knows she wished her brother could have enjoyed this ride with her. Derrick loved the sunrise.

Although Amara tried to talk with him each day, she hadn't seen him in over a week. As much as she wanted to see him, she had avoided the therapeutic center for another reason: money. Certainly some of the staff would approach her about the mounting bill.

"How's my little baby bro doing today?" Amara greeted Derrick with a hug of his husky shoulders. Sitting in his bed, he embraced her heartily. When they parted, he revealed a grin so huge and deep, it looked carved into his round face. Amara was ecstatic to see him so happy. What's more, he seemed heavier with each visit. The injuries and mental stress from the accident had originally caused him to lose his appetite and become thin. Prior to the accident, he was big-boned, as their mother used to chant proudly.

"You look good, and like your old self!"

Derrick lit up even more. "I feel good and like my old self. The doctor said if I keep up with my therapy like I have been, I might be walking out of here within the next few months."

"That's what I dream of," Amara said, easing down on the side of his bed.

Derrick patted her hand. "It's coming, sis. With God's help, it's coming. So what have you been up to? And when is Terrence coming back to see me? He's cool."

Amara maintained her calm expression as she responded to her brother with fabrication after fabrication. How could she tell him that Terrence had not only broken her heart, but also destroyed her so much that she had the misfortune of being evicted from her home? Keeping his stress level low was crucial in his recovery. Because Derrick bonded with Terrence so well, it would have torn him apart to know how Terrence had mistreated her. As well, Amara didn't want him to worry about her struggle to pay for his medical care. It was so much easier to let Derrick believe Terrence treated her wonderfully and finances were plentiful.

After Amara's pleasant visit with Derrick was over, she walked down the center's hallway with an uplifted spirit. During those moments of laughing and talking with her brother, she had almost forgotten her troubles. As she headed toward the center's billing office, she had no choice but to confront her woes. With knots forming in her stomach, Amara walked into the office. Moments later, she sat before the director of the facility.

"Ms. Hart," Ms. Eagleton said without the slightest warmth, "we need at least half of the amount owed, or you will have to make other arrangements for your brother. I'm sorry."

Amara was sorry, too, as she drove a dark, lonesome highway. The feeling caused her to drive aimlessly for hours after she left the center. She was sorry for dating her married boss, a man married to a mentally frail woman. Was her current predicament punishment for dating such a man? The questions were a waste of time. She needed cash, lots of it, and she knew of one way to get it.

Within seconds, Amara drove along another road. Sooner than she desired, she arrived at a two-story, Tudor-style mansion. Hesitantly, she stepped out of her car and rang the bell. After the fourth ring, the door opened.

Wearing business slacks and a shirt that looked a bit rumpled, Terrence drew back with such shock that it took a moment before he smiled. "So what can I do for you tonight, beautiful lady?"

Chapter Five

Amara hesitated. "I thought about your offer."

The words brought an overjoyed expression to Terrence's face. He grasped Amara's hand, gently guiding her inside his home. While he shut the door and secured it, she walked through the foyer. When she entered the living room, a quick scan of it showed nothing had changed. Gold ornaments accentuated posh modern décor in hues of champagne and bone. A berry scented candle burned. A Prince slow jam played at a low volume on the stereo. Terrence gestured for her to sit down on his sofa.

Amara strode across the thick carpet and took a seat. "I'm sorry to come by so late."

Terrence sat next to her, his expression now serious. "I want you to know that you still have an open invitation to come by anytime."

"Terrence, I don't want you to get the wrong idea."

"What idea is that?"

"That I came by for...well you know."

"Because you still want me like I want you," Terrence replied ardently.

"That's not why..." She heard a bump upstairs, which drew her attention in its direction. Swiftly, she focused back on Terrence. "That's not why I'm here."

"You said you've been thinking about my offer. Is that the offer for us to be together again, or the one about the job? Because I know you wouldn't drive all the way here tonight to turn me down."

"It's the offer about the job."

Terrence nodded. "If you want it, you got it."

"I do want it."

"Then it's yours."

"Thank you," Amara said, hoping she hadn't made a mistake.

"No, thank you. You were an awesome agent who brought in great revenue. I was foolish to fire you."

Amara felt like giving him an earful about how foolish he was. Instead, she held her tongue-lashing and then ignored several more thumps from upstairs. Without a doubt, Terrence had company.

"So does this mean we're starting over with a clean slate?" he asked.

"I guess it does," she replied, unable to shake the uneasiness she felt about her decision.

"Are we starting over with everything?" His gold-brown eyes focused on her lips.

"No, not that."

Terrence nodded. "That's cool."

"Is it, Terrence? Because I can't go through all that stuff with you again. I need a job, and I'm ready to work really hard for you."

"I know you will."

"Then can I have your word that I can be your colleague and employee without you expecting more? I want to be treated like any other real estate agent in the office. I don't want to be harassed."

"And you won't be. We can work together without being lovers. But at the same time, you have to give me time with my feelings. I can't just turn off the way I feel about you. I can't stop looking at you the way I do. I can't stop wanting what we once had. And there are times I might slip up and express myself. But if you don't want to be back where we were, I give you my word that I won't give you problems. Trust me."

Amara studied him as he spoke those last words before more noises from upstairs distracted her. She gazed up again and this time saw a woman at the top of the stairwell. Clutching the rail, she appeared shapely, biscuit-colored, with a short, brown afro. She looked vaguely familiar.

Though, Amara didn't question if she was Michelle, Terrence's wife, and had suddenly returned home. After she learned of his marriage, she had scoured the internet for information about her and came across numerous photos of Terrence escorting Michelle to various events. No, this was someone else geared up to be Terrence's lover.

Amara watched her step down a few stairs into better view. Clearly, she wanted to flaunt her black, chiffon negligee, which exposed all of her curves and then some.

"Terry, where are the matches? The candles blew out." She stared at Amara.

"In the left night table drawer," Terrence replied hastily.

The woman continued to stare at Amara.

In fact, her staring made Amara so uncomfortable she stood and shifted her focus to Terrence. "I'm leaving now. So you go enjoy your evening."

Terrence shot his guest an annoyed look for staring, which made her vanish. Then he eased in front of Amara. "You don't have to leave. Let's finish here."

"No, I need to get home."

Amara walked to the front door. Terrence accompanied her. Before she stepped outside, he cornered her.

"You don't have to worry about her," he spoke in a hushed tone.

"Terrence, I'm not all up in your business."

"I know you're not, but I just wanted you to know. She is just a woman that's here. But she's not in here." He grasped Amara's hand and laid her palm against his chest. It beat so madly, it stunned Amara.

Terrence studied her astonishment. "That's right. You still do that to me. But I won't push. Even if we're not together, I'm just excited that you're back in my life. It's enough for me. It's enough. Now, I'll see you in the morning at work."

"Thank you, Terrence."

"No, thank you." He opened the door to let her out.

By the time Terrence reached his bedroom, Sandy stood in front of the mirror lightly blotting her flawless makeup with a sponge. "What did she want?"

"It was business." Terrence unbuttoned his white, cotton shirt, which Sandy had begun taking off before Amara interrupted them. "Nothing more."

"What type of business?"

"She works for me. She's one of my agents."

"Oh, really. So why couldn't she wait to tell you at work? Why does your ex-girlfriend have to stop by at this hour if it's just business?"

"How did you know she was my ex?"

"You brought her to the restaurant where I worked a few times. Back then, I was just an admirer of yours, finding you and your guest the perfect table. It was obvious you were involved. You couldn't keep your hands off of her."

A tiny smile curled Terrence's lips. "That just shows that I had a life with someone else before you. But now, you're here with me."

Sandy swung around from the mirror, her heart-shaped face half-angry, half-vulnerable. Brushing past Terrence, she headed into the bathroom. As he continued to disrobe, he delighted in her jealousy. He knew it wouldn't hinder what would take place between them shortly. He had recently moved Sandy and her two young daughters into one of the swanky penthouses Bryce and he had recently purchased for investment properties. Additionally, he wooed her with fine clothing, jewelry, and other possessions.

Would she actually withhold sex and lose all of that? Especially since prior to meeting him, she hosted at a seafood restaurant and struggled to pay her bills. Terrence adored the control money had over people. What's more, he felt certain he could have made love to Amara in the living room, before Sandy's eyes, and Sandy would have forgiven him and would continue giving him sweet loving—because the almighty dollar always ruled.

Before long, Terrence sat in bed naked, a burgundy satin sheet covering him from the waist down. Sandy came out of the bathroom. As she walked toward the bed, he admired her curvaceous legs and the luscious breasts that teased him through the sheer black fabric. Without a doubt, she was a stunner who possessed all those lush curves that made him go crazy about a woman. Even so, he couldn't deny what he felt. A part of him wished Amara wore that negligee and was slipping into the silken sheets with him instead of Sandy.

"There's something in your eyes, Terry. It makes me feel like

45

you're thinking about her."

Terrence ignored Sandy's words, easing atop her and palming her breasts. "I'm going for what I want."

She drew a breath, as his touch became bolder. "Don't play games with my heart."

"I'm here with you, now." Terrence caressed open the top of the flimsy negligee and kissed her breasts. They were more than a mouthful, just as he liked them. Tantalizing, they smelled like a mixture of baby powder and lavender. "You smell so good, baby."

"Don't try to change the subject," she slurred her eyes opening and closing lazily. "You're not right."

"I'm right. And I know what you want, don't I?"

Terrence heard no response from Sandy. She was too busy moaning as he stroked her nipples and eased her out of her negligee. When she was finally bare, his hands caressed her, particularly between her warm, silky thighs. Throughout every second, Terrence's erection grew to explosive excitement.

Placing his fingers between her tight, wet folds, he played with her clitoris. Feeling her tremble and beg for him to please her fully, Terrence needed no more encouragement than to do what he wanted to do all along, to give her every steel inch of himself without all the frills of foreplay, or for that matter, without even kissing. He wanted sex right now and hard.

Sandy squeezed his thick, long penis into a condom. Terrence pushed her firm thighs far apart and placed himself between them, pushing inside of her as far as he could go. She moaned loudly. Once he began moving, pumping hard, he knew hit her hot zone. Sandy lost her mind, screeching to the top of her lungs, while clinging to his broad, sweaty back.

Lost in the heavenly feeling, Terrence grabbed her legs and thrust harder and harder, so hard he himself couldn't control the outcries of satisfaction that came out of his mouth. Nor could he control the semen spilling from his body, or even the thoughts that swept through his mind. For each time he closed his eyes, he imagined moving within Amara's luscious, drenched walls.

Moments later, they were spent and soon sleeping. He dreamed about Amara and then had another about his wife, Michelle. Terrence woke and gazed at Sandy sleeping next to him and started to wake her for more fun. Images of Amara stopped him. The beautiful woman in his dream, who had been downstairs hours ago, was back in his life again. Of course, he intended to make her his. But this time, he would celebrate success. After all, soon there would be no wife for Amara to worry her pretty head about. He would be free of Michelle.

Michelle Johnson walked away from the sanitarium room's small, dark window and shuffled toward the bed across the room. Feeling more imprisoned than treated for mental illness, she caught a look of herself in the mirror. The broken woman reflected back, made her step closer for a better inspection.

She did not resemble herself. Her waist-length, naturally sandy hair had become thin, stringy, and looked tousled even when she brushed it. Her Asian-like eyes had dark circles beneath them. Her caramel colored complexion looked dull, and her plump, curvy figure that used to make men drool and call her Queen Latifah's twin, appeared shapeless.

Shaking her head and fighting back tears, she dragged herself away from the mirror just as the night nurse entered her room.

"Mrs. Johnson," she said, tugging up her outdated glasses at the middle. "Ready for your medicine?"

"Never."

"Mrs. Johnson, please don't make this difficult. I'm just doing my job." Nurse Henderson handed Michelle the tiny, white cup containing the strange smelling pill.

Michelle flashed a hostile look, took the cup, turned it up to her mouth, and swallowed. She had long ago convinced Nurse Henderson that she could take her pills without water. With her work completed, the nurse smiled and left the room. Michelle hurried into the bathroom, spit the pill in the toilet and flushed.

As she watched the water swirl, whisking the drug away, Michelle acknowledged that she hadn't been the nicest person in the world in her thirty-eight years. In fact, she had been a spoiled, selfish,

47

rich brat most of the time. Still, no one deserved what she had endured in recent years. The hospital wouldn't get away with it. Most of all, Terrence wouldn't get away with it.

Bryce sat in his office, sorting through paperwork when he heard TJ Realty's outside buzzer. At shortly after 8:00 am, it was too early for the staff to come to work. Wondering if FedEx was delivering the new fax machine he ordered, he pressed the intercom.

"TJ Realty, may I help you?"

"Bryce, is that you?"

"Amara?" Recognizing her voice, his eyes widened and his voice rose.

"Yes, I'm reporting to work," Amara said with a chuckle. "Let me in."

Within minutes, Bryce reared back in his chair in amazement as he listened to heels clacking against the tiled parts of the office.

"I'm in here," he yelled, beckoning Amara to his office.

Soon Amara sashayed through the door, wearing a navy colored suit with a white trimmed collar. High-heeled matching pumps complimented the outfit. She was stunning and was a beautiful morning surprise he had not expected. A subtle strawberry-like scent drifted in with her presence. It filled Bryce with the desire to get as close to her as he could, but he controlled himself.

He offered her a thick-cushioned, gray chair, which she gladly accepted. "So you changed your mind about coming back to work here?"

"I sure did."

"Tee didn't tell me you were joining our team again."

"Probably because he found out late last night. I stopped by his house and told him I'd reconsidered his offer."

"By his house?" he asked, wondering if the visit was solely about business.

"It was hard to swallow my pride. But I'm back." She stood. "And I'm ready to start. But why are we the only two here?"

"Because I always come in early. The staff comes in at 10:00

am now."

"Oh."

"But your being here early is fine. I can help you get settled."

"Sounds great."

Smiling, he stared at her silently.

"Why are you looking at me like that?"

"Because I'm so happy you're back. It's going to be great working with you."

"I feel the same way."

As Bryce began to re-familiarize Amara with her responsibilities, more than once he resisted the urge to give her a long, body-clinging hug and show her how thrilled he really was to see her. She had stayed on his mind constantly since their last encounter. Now, he would have the pleasure of seeing her almost every day. Then again, so would Terrence. He wondered what other matters they had come to agreement on when she visited Terrence at his house. Since Terrence claimed he would soon be single, would they rekindle their hot affair? If they did, could he handle it?

Chapter Six

By 10:30, all of TJ Realty's employees sat at their desks with coffee, donuts, blueberry muffins, or whatever indulgence they enjoyed to begin their day. Once Terrence arrived, he welcomed Amara back and let the other agents know she had rejoined their team. While he escorted her around the office and introduced her to the numerous new agents, she was amazed to see how much the company had grown.

"Business is certainly booming," Amara remarked, returning to her desk.

Terrence shuffled next to her. "I told you so."

"Congrats."

"Hey, having my man Bryce on board with me made all the difference. The man is a genius, you know."

Amara glanced at Bryce. He stood across the room, speaking with an agent. Amara scooted down in her seat and switched her attention to the screen in front of her. "I should set up my agent web page now."

"I can help you with that." Terrence bent down, leaning over her shoulder.

Their faces were so close that Amara inhaled his citrus-based cologne. She shifted away from him in protest to his unsubtle closeness. "I should have brought in a photo from home for the page," she said.

"Not necessary. We have an outstanding photographer to take our agent's photos now. I'm sure he will be pleased to take yours. I used to love photographing you, your eyes, your lips…and your body." Amara glimpsed aside at him to caution him about flirting. It made her have second thoughts about her decision. How many times during the day would she have to deal with Terrence behaving this way?

At one point, his gaze even lowered to her lips as if he wanted to kiss her. If he had tried it, he would have been sadly disappointed.

Though, she did hunger for a kiss too--a kiss from another man who wasn't too faraway. However, Amara shook off the thought. She was at TJ to do a job, not get a man. "So what's uh…" she said, "what's the first thing I should do despite not having my photo yet?"

After Bryce finished a conversation with an employee, he headed to his office. Noticing Terrence leaning over Amara's shoulder, and pointing out something to her on the computer screen, he felt at odds. On one hand, he had encouraged her to accept the job at TJ Realty. On the other hand, he suddenly wrestled with mixed emotions about her return. Terrence and she seemed like they weren't at odds anymore. Had Amara decided to become his lover again, too?

Eventually settling behind his desk, Bryce's mind fought to concentrate on work. When Terrence entered his office, looking happier than he had in a long time, Bryce braced himself to hear about their revived relationship.

"Isn't it great having Amara back?" Terrence plopped down on the black, leather sofa in Bryce's office and stretched his arm along the top of it.

"Wonderful," Bryce agreed, questioning if Terrence and Amara had rekindled their romance.

"Yes indeed. And she's already on top of her game. She's meeting with a few sellers this afternoon. One of the homes is that mansion on Culver Hill."

"Nice. Pricey, too."

"Oh, yeah. It's almost as if Amara never left. I was foolish to let her go."

"You damn sure were. What did you do to get her back?" He couldn't shake the idea that they might be involved once again. "I mean…is there anything else to this?"

"I just presented the offer. Her situation dictated the rest."

"So are you two…" Bryce swallowed. "Back together?"

"I wish."

Bryce secretly exhaled. "Well, don't mess up. Just remain a friend and keep everything professional."

"Of course I will."

"I mean it. She's talented. She can really bring sales to this firm."

"You don't have to convince me."

"So it's going to be all business?"

Terrence snickered. "Man, you know me."

"Sure do."

"Then you know I never give up."

Bryce started to respond, but Terrence received a call on his cell. Their chat concluded, as Terrence took the call outside the office, Bryce sat fuming at Terrence's scheming. What was so bad about Terrence giving up on her and letting her do her job? Then again, he knew the answer. Terrence never gave up when he wanted something—or someone. But he wouldn't allow his old friend to hire Amara and fire her when she didn't hop in his bed. He wasn't just starting at the firm like the last time when she worked there and unaware of what was really happening. He was a full partner with his eye and finger on every aspect of the business. Ensuring Amara had a stress free work environment would be his major business.

By week's end, Amara proved that she hadn't lost her touch as a top selling agent. Not only had she made such successful listing presentations with sellers, she also had secured several homes to sell, and sold the mansion on Culver Hill, a highly lucrative property.

Before taking off to a meeting, Terrence shared the good news with Bryce. After Bryce wrapped up some calls, he made his way to Amara's desk.

She skimmed over a loan application, but put it aside when she saw him. "Did you hear about my good news?"

His eyes twinkled with his excitement. "Sure did. Congratulations."

"Thanks. It feels good to be back, doing what I love."

"You're doing it up right, too." He delighted in her lovely smile. "Why don't you have lunch with me to celebrate?"

"With my boss?"

"With your boss."

"Well, I can't refuse my boss, can I?"

Bryce chuckled, helped her into her jacket. Soon they were off.

The Blue Nile Grill, an eatery located in Ocean City, was a posh-looking establishment, decorated with dim lights, and classic décor. The window wall granted an admirer a breathtaking view of the Atlantic. A restaurant known to stir the salivary glands with just the mention of its name, the Blue Nile Grill boasted a variety of exotic, mouthwatering dishes.

Seated at table beside a ceiling-to-floor window filled with a marine blue sea, Amara faced Bryce and marveled at a display that looked like dinner instead of lunch. From the Cajun duck, to the pineapple shrimp, to the caramelized vegetables, to the bacon wrapped rice, to the sea scallops with porcini mushrooms, to all the scrumptious other dishes that decorated the table, she made sure she tasted everything.

Bryce grinned as she wolfed down the various types of cuisine.

"What's so funny?" Amara asked playfully.

"You. I like a woman who doesn't play around with food. I'm enjoying watching you eat your meal."

"You are?" Amara was amused.

"Oh, yeah." He stuck a forkful of duck in his mouth.

"Well, normally, I keep an eye on what I eat. Like every other woman I know, I try to watch my figure. But hey, I'm celebrating. This all is too good and I'm hungry."

"So eat up. But you don't need to watch your figure."

"And why do you say that?" She sipped a fruity, frothy drink.

"Because everything about you is just perfect."

Amara noted how his eyes clung to hers with those words. "Thank you. It means a lot since you've seen me…."

"Naked?" Swiftly his gaze dropped below her neck, and then met her eyes.

Amara squirmed in her chair. "Yes, naked."

"I guess it was easy for you to get the job at the university as an artist's model."

"I interviewed, but thank God they didn't ask me to take off my clothes for the interview."

"So do you think you'll ever model again for a portrait like that?"

"Not for the public. Maybe for my man."

Bryce's thick brows rose. "Oh, so you're seeing someone?"

"No." She paused as she chewed a shrimp. "I mean when I do start seeing someone. Are you seeing someone?"

Bryce poured French dressing on his salad. "I date sometimes."

"Anything serious?"

"No. My parents ask me that all the time. But I haven't met anyone with whom I feel a true connection. And I haven't met anyone who would pose for such a sexy portrait for me." Smiling devilishly, Bryce rubbed his chin. "That man in your future is going to be very lucky. Very, very lucky."

There was a long silence as Amara mused about what he said. She watched Bryce chewing his food. She took in his sleek, dark skin, sparkling, seductive eyes, and inviting lips before her gaze lowered to those massive shoulders covered sexily in a charcoal gray suit. It all made her long to see him again clad in only a towel—and less.

Yet it was more than this man's gorgeous appearance that captivated her. It was the man himself. He had been so kind to her that she wanted to do something, which would make him feel very, very lucky. "I'll pose for you."

Bryce stopped chewing and gawked at her. "What did you say?"

"I said I'll pose for you."

"Pose for me how?"

"In whatever way you want. Like I posed in the class, if you want."

Bryce stared into her eyes, excitement radiating from his, until suddenly his gaze rose above and behind Amara. Following his line of vision, she looked over her shoulder. To her shock, Carlyn stood by their table. A male guest accompanied her.

"Hello," she greeted them both cheerily.

Bryce smiled. "How are you?"

"I'm great. I've been promoted to manager at a hotel. Life is too good."

"That's fantastic. I'm glad to see things working out so well. Would you and your guest like a seat?"

"No, we have a table," Carlyn replied with a glimpse at her friend. "I just wanted to stop by to say hello to you and my roommate."

Bryce's head tilted with surprise. He looked at Amara. "You two are roommates?"

"Temporarily."

"Yes, it's temp," Carlyn added. "Anyway, enjoy your eats."

Bryce nodded. "You, too."

"See you," Amara threw in.

As Carlyn walked away, Amara observed her closely. The hostess escorted her and her companion to a table. Nevertheless, Jamie's cousin's attention remained on Amara and Bryce once they were seated. Amara couldn't understand Carlyn's preoccupation with her life. She looked forward to moving out of Jamie's house, mostly because of her.

"Where were we?" Ignoring his food, Bryce leaned toward her with an anxious expression.

"I don't remember," Amara teased.

"Oh, yes, you do. We were talking about you posing for me. Posing any way I want. Posing like you posed in my class."

"We were?" Her voice was full of playfulness.

He laughed. "Okay, you want to be like that and get a brother crazy-excited. We'll leave the subject for now and get back to work. But I'm not forgetting the offer."

Amara offered him a sensuous smile.

Less than an hour after Amara and Bryce returned to the office, Terrence called her into his office and closed the door.

"I want to thank you for doing such a great job," he said, facing her across his office lounge table.

"You thanked me already, Terrence."

"No, I would like to really thank you. How about dinner at your favorite spot?"

Amara shook her head. "That's not a good idea."

"Oh, come on."

"No, really. I'd rather not."

"It's just dinner between friends, or a boss and employee, or whatever you want to call it. Hell, we have lots to celebrate. You came in here and turned this place out with a sale of a major property."

"I'm happy to do that, for you and myself. But no dinner. I really want to work with you. Please let me do that hassle free."

"I don't want you to feel hassled."

"Then don't push, please."

He expelled a long, deep sigh. "All right. I guess I have to except a no."

"Great."

"But is it because of the woman you saw at my place the other night? Because I told you, we're not serious. She's like a buddy."

"It doesn't matter. I'm here just to do a great job for this company, without any complications. Now, let me get back to work."

"Cool. Go do your thing."

Amara walked out of Terrence's office, closing the door behind her. Beside it, Bryce's office door stood open. From his desk chair, he eyed Amara with a mischievous grin that let her know he hadn't forgotten the portrait. She offered him a spicy grin and kept on going.

Chapter Seven

The super busy agents of TJ Realty had checked out for the day. Placing important documents in his briefcase to analyze at home, Bryce intended to do the same. Furthermore, he couldn't wait to kick back and rest before his expected guests arrived for the evening. Mostly, he wanted to relax and think about what was happening between Amara and himself. Their lunchtime discussion stimulated him.

Was she kidding about the nude portrait? Was she willing to come to his place, strip completely naked, so he could paint her? Just the image of her nudeness filled him with such lust, he hardened as if she stood before him, willing and ready at that precise moment. Going over their conversation in his head, he finished packing his attaché. That is, until he heard a crash from inside Terrence's office.

"What's that?" he yelled, running toward the commotion.

When he ran in the office, he saw that Terrence had thrown a flowerpot against the wall. Now, he rifled through files.

"What's going on?" Bryce asked as he walked into the room, looking from the broken flowerpot pieces to Terrence now rifling through his files. "Why did you lose your temper like that?"

"It's nothing, man. Go on home." Terrence continued rummaging through the files.

"I'm not going anywhere until I know what's going on with you."

"It's nothing I said."

"It is something. The last time you went loony in here, Amara had cut you off."

Terrence stopped and looked up at him.

"Oh no. You messed up, didn't you?"

"Man, stop getting dramatic. Amara and I are cool."

"So why did you go off like that?"

"Because."

"Because what?"

Terrence closed the file cabinet. "I just wanted to take her to dinner."

"And?"

"She turned me down."

"So."

"So I wanted to celebrate. She comes back here and in her first week makes a grand slam. I just wanted to thank her."

Sourly, Bryce pursed his lips. "Tee, come on. You know you wanted more."

"So what the hell if I did?"

"She just wants her job. She's been through a lot. She lost her place. Her brother's recovering from serious injuries. And she has financial problems. Give her a break."

Sighing, Terrence sat back on the edge of his desk. "Man, I know I should. But every time I'm around her or just think about her being here again, it just does something to me. She gets me so damn worked up. I just want to get her in my bed and make us both climb the walls. You know how it is, when you know how good something is. We were so good together. The best damn sex I ever had."

Bryce's jaw twitched. Terrence's last sentence conjured up a visual image he couldn't stand. Terrence and Amara couldn't be intimate again. He wasn't the man for her. He couldn't make her happy. "Is that all you want from Amara—sex?"

"Hell no. We had something special. Our personalities clicked. Our everything clicked. Man, I love that woman. I thought I stopped, but I still do. That's why I really have to take care of Michelle now."

"Take care of her?" Bryce's eyes narrowed. "What do you mean by that?"

"You know. The divorce."

"While she is still being treated at a mental facility?"

"Look, there is no telling how long she's going to be there. Why should I have to put my life on hold when we were about to divorce before she even went there?"

"Tee, do the right thing."

"You mean pretend that I love her? Or be noble like you. Man, I could never do what you did."

"Forget about me. We're talking about you and your wife. Remember there is a person there, a person with a heart and a soul. You just don't throw her away like she's nothing."

"You want me to welcome her home when all I can think about is making love to another woman?"

"No," he said, feeling more and more uncomfortable hearing about Terrence's desire for Amara. "I just want you to do things the right way. You married Michelle and shared your life with her. Treat her with respect. Make sure she's solid and whole before you end it. I know how much Michelle loved you. Sometimes I wonder if you ever loved her."

"Of course I did. But in no way does it compare to what I feel for Amara."

On and on the conversation went about Michelle and Amara. By the time Bryce drove home, he felt exhausted by their discussion. Trying to convince Terrence to see his way of thinking wasn't all that wore him out. No, his own demons wrestled within him, as well. He should have told Terrence to leave Amara alone for her peace of mind and the good of the company. Instead, he'd chewed him out because he couldn't stop wanting her for himself.

Sauntering into Jamie's house, Amara's mind raced with the week's beautiful surprises. Her big sale topped the list. Also at that pinnacle was her time spent with Bryce. Lunch with him had been entertaining. Dangling the proposition of a nude portrait before Bryce made her feel flirtatious and alive. She couldn't stop smiling as she passed through the living room.

Carlyn lounged on the sofa, watching the soap channel on cable. A small, wicker basket full of Buffalo wings and French fries sat on the wood coffee table. The well-seasoned smell of the wings made Amara realize she was famished.

"Seemed like you enjoyed lunch," Carlyn commented.

"Yes, lunch with Bryce was fun. We were celebrating my first sale since being back. I sold a mansion on Culver Hill."

"Wow, those are expensive. I guess that commission will help you get a place."

"It's a blessing. Anyway, have a good evening." Amara climbed the stairs.

"How does Terrence feel about what's going on?"

Amara froze at the words spoken to her back. "Excuse me." Frowning, she turned on the step. "What do you mean, what's going on?"

"I'm talking about Bryce. I was just curious about how Terrence feels about you and Bryce getting cozy at lunch. I'm sure he didn't hire you again just for you to become a little too friendly with his best friend. It didn't seem like you two were just talking about business when I saw you today."

Amara took a deep breath, trying not to let this woman anger her. Obviously, Carlyn still harbored strong feelings for Terrence. Otherwise, why would this concern her? "We weren't getting cozy. We were just having lunch to celebrate my sale. And as far as what we were talking about, it's our own business, isn't it?"

Carlyn's thin lips curled in a sly grin. "If you say so."

Amara shook her head at the busybody and continued up the stairs to her room. Once she settled down, she knocked on Jamie's door.

"Come in."

Sprawled across the bed, Jamie tucked a bookmark on the page of her latest romance novel. Setting the book on her night table, she sat up. "How was your day, lady?"

"Very interesting."

"Oh, really now. Make yourself comfortable and tell me all about it." Jamie patted a spot on her flowery bedspread.

Amara plunked down next to her. "I had lunch with Bryce to celebrate my sale."

"That sounds nice."

"It was more than nice. The food was fantastic." Her face glowed as she spoke. "And the conversation was something else."

"Like what?"

Amara smiled, thinking of her proposal to Bryce. He looked and sounded so excited about it. She wished to see and hear his excitement again. "Well," she answered Jamie, "I told him I would pose for a private portrait for him, in whatever way he wanted."

Jamie's raised a high arched brow. "What?"

Amara nodded. "Uh huh, yes I did."

"Girl, what's gotten into you?"

"Just feeling happy for the first time in a long time, and it's due mostly to him. It means a lot when the world just seems so dark, and someone extends genuine kindness. He has no idea what he did for me. He restored my faith in people."

"So you want to strip and let the man paint you?" Jamie sat up straighter.

"It's not just that. It's that he helped me so much. And we were sitting and talking about portraits like that." Amara ran her fingers through her hair. "He said how lucky my man would be to have me do that for him. So, I just thought what better way could I show my gratitude?"

"Mm, mm, mm, girl, he's getting you hot, isn't he?"

Amara tapped Jamie's arm, but she knew Jamie saw through her. "Oh, stop."

"Stop nothing. That man has you on fire and you're looking for any reason to give him some loving. Well, like I said before, let him help himself."

Amara cracked up at her friend's comment. As she sobered, she realized Jamie had spoken her heart. Desire filled her each time she thought of Bryce Davidson. She wanted to see the hunger in his eyes when he looked at her naked body. More than that, she ached to feel him so very deeply inside of her. But suddenly, a thought dimmed the fantasy. "I can't do it."

"Why not?"

"First off, I don't believe in having sex with a guy just because I'm horny for him."

Jamie gave her a pointed look. "This will be your first time then. Get over your self and get some of that fine man."

"Jamie, I'm serious. Terrence and Bryce have TJ Realty together and other investments." She stretched out on her side, leaning on her elbow. "They're best friends."

"Didn't you say that Terrence has a new woman?"

"He told me she's not important to him. Today he wanted so badly to take me to dinner. When I turned him down, he almost looked like he did when he unleashed his wrath on me before."

"Girl, you are going to have to decide if Terrence is going rule your life. Or are you going to be with the man you truly want?"

Jamie's latter words spun in Amara's head so much she found herself driving to Bryce's estate. Of course, she had the perfect excuse. She intended to say she needed some outfits she had left in his garage. Or perhaps she could even bring up the portrait again and let him begin to paint her.

At Bryce's mansion, Amara rang the bell. Soon he opened the door and looked pleasantly surprised. Amara felt ecstatic at the sight of him, as well. Until that is, a woman walked up behind him. She sported an adorable short, shaggy cut hairstyle and had an athletic build, and creamy rich brown skin.

"You said the boy you mentor and his mom are coming by tonight?" she asked, gazing at Amara. "Is this her?"

"No. This is my friend and colleague, Amara. Amara, please come on in."

Amara didn't budge from the front doorstep. "Oh, no, I'm not staying. I just wanted to get some outfits for work out of your garage."

"Sure, it's open. I'll walk over with you."

"That's not necessary. Have a good evening." Amara rushed toward the garage, wanting to punch herself for dropping by unexpectedly. As she searched for her clothes through the numerous boxes, she felt silly for interrupting Bryce's apparent romantic rendezvous. Certainly, a sweet, gorgeous man like him wouldn't be alone every night. He even admitted that he dated during their lunch together that afternoon.

When Amara heard heavy footsteps entering the garage, she

turned around to meet his gaze. "I'm sorry I interrupted you and your date. I had no right to just drop by."

"You have every right, because I say so. And she's not a date."

"You don't have to explain."

"No, really. She's not."

"Then…then who is she?"

"My…my sister-in-law."

Amara's mouth dropped open with speechless shock. "You're married, too?"

Chapter Eight

"I was married. My wife is surely now an angel in heaven."

Amara clutched her chest and hid her relief. "Oh no."

"She was the friend who wanted me to pursue my art, the one we talked about in the car."

"I could tell she was someone special to you," she said, her head spinning with this news.

"We weren't married long, but long enough for her to be happy before..."

The words and his suddenly intense expression intrigued her. Amara wanted to hear more. Unfortunately, she heard his sister-in-law approaching and calling, "Bryce?"

"Yes?"

The woman hurried into the garage. "The boy you mentor and his mother are up at the house."

"Right." Bryce glimpsed his watch, and then looked at Amara. "Will you excuse me?"

"Sure. I'll get my things and see you tomorrow."

Hours later, Bryce finished scheduling the upcoming summer activities with the youngster he mentored. For three years, he had been part of a program to help boys gain self-esteem and career guidance. It gave him an overwhelming feeling of purpose to help a child who had no role model to navigate this complicated world. Bryce had urged Terrence to become a mentor also, but he declined. Terrence claimed he had no time for kids. He boasted that he reserved his time for making money and having lots of sex.

During the time the boy and his mother had visited, Bryce's sister-in-law, Lynne, went elsewhere in the house to leave them alone.

He encouraged her to give herself a tour of the place since this was her first time in this particular home. When his guests left, Lynne rejoined Bryce in the living room. Strolling around it, she admired his many pictures and sipped a margarita.

"I always liked that you loved to have a lot of pictures around you."

"Hey, family is important. But so are friends." He picked up a photo from a shelf. His mother, father and two of his four brothers smiled back at him. He missed being with them in Chicago. Then again, if he hadn't left, he wouldn't have met the woman who was getting under his skin like no one he's ever encountered.

"Hey, look at this." Lynne picked up a picture from the mantle and placed it in front of him. His beloved Kimberly glowed. "She was all freckles and all smiles," Lynne said.

With a sad look, Bryce stared at the photo for a long while, and then said, "She looks happy."

"She was. You had just proposed to her in this picture. What woman wouldn't be happy? I certainly would. You're a good man, Bryce. Everyone on the block knew you would turn out to be that way when you grew up. My folks used to talk about how much manners you had. But my sister and I used to just talk about how cute you were." She shot him a playfully seductive look.

Bryce missed her flirtatiousness, distracted by memories of Kimberly. Finally, he looked at Lynne, almost as if he had just returned from somewhere faraway. "So how are your folks doing?" He gestured for her to sit on the sofa, and then sat down himself.

"They're all right." Lynne joined him on the couch. "But they told me I better not pass through Maryland without seeing their favorite son-in-law."

Bryce grinned. "I'm their only son-in-law."

"That's true," Lynne said with a chuckle. "But they do truly love you. You made Kim's dying wish come true. She wanted to be married like in a fairy tale before she died. So you married her and made her a princess. I don't know if I have any male friends who would have done that for me."

"She deserved to be happy. Ever since I knew her, she struggled with that weak heart, smiling even when I knew she wanted to cry. Sometimes life isn't fair; good people suffer and it makes you wonder." He shook his head, not wanting to discuss it any further. "Let's change the subject. So how do you like being the fashion buyer for this big chain?"

"I truly love it, but it does get lonely. It's hard to sustain a relationship when I'm working crazy hours and doing so much traveling."

"But I'm sure you meet lots of interesting men."

"They're okay. They're just not special. They're not like you." She stared at Bryce so hard and long, he felt uncomfortable and looked away.

When Lynne left, Bryce showered and lay in bed, nude. He felt tired after his hectic day at work and the planning of the youth activities program, but couldn't go to sleep. Thoughts of Amara floated through his mind. He closed his eyes and pictured them in his bedroom.

He imagined Amara plopped back on the bed, smiling seductively and bouncing on the mattress. At the same time, he lit strawberry-scented candles enclosed in rounded holders on the nightstands. To set the mood further, he rummaged through his music collection for the perfect song. He found the old O'Jays' classic "Stairway To Heaven" and slipped it in the CD player. It sounded just as sexy, as he longed to be with Amara.

Soon Bryce caressed her face and mingled his fingers in her long, cinnamon colored locks. He could tell her body heated from that alone. When he finally eased his muscular body on top of Amara and kissed her, she felt and tasted more luscious than he imagined.

Taking his time to drain out every drop of pleasure, his tongue slid in and out of her mouth. At the same instant, he reached down in her pants and his fingers treated her wet warmth to the same erotic motion of his kiss. He could tell that her lower body became taut with a pressure that ached for some of his hard sweet relief. Anxiously, she unzipped his pants and gripped what she needed. Kissing deeper and hungrier, they stripped each other naked.

She stared at him, loving what she saw. He did the same as she lay back on the bed. When he couldn't take staring without having her, he kissed her. He kissed every feature of her beautiful face. He kissed behind her ears and the length of her neck. He kissed the healthy swell of her cleavage, her entire breasts and her pointed nipples. She moaned as if the kissing were almost painful, but as he looked up in her eyes, he saw how much it turned on her on and how much more she desired him.

He went lower, christening her ribs and belly with his lips and tongue. Then he skipped the middle, and thrilled her toes, ankles, and legs. When finally he returned to the middle of her, he could tell she was ready as he was for the main course. He moved her thighs far apart and stuck his finger in her wet vagina, playing with her clit until she trembled from the pleasure. But there was more. He positioned his face there, and stuck an eager tongue inside.

Miles away Amara lay in her bed fantasizing too—fantasizing about Bryce. In her dreams, his tongue had sent her clitoris into a frenzy, making her orgasm unlike she had experienced before. And just when she believed she couldn't feel anymore, he brought his penis toward her wet, throbbing opening. He was gleaming. He was strong and he was huge.

Amara couldn't believe she was about to feel Bryce inside of her. With it, she loved that starving way he stared in her eyes and at her body. She couldn't get over how his lips pampered her, kissed her all over, making her feel loved and desired. Then in one perfect moment, he opened her up with his fingers and made the way for his huge penis. It pushed so heavenly and deeply inside of her, she whimpered with delight.

Breathing in his worked-up scent, kissing his lips, and holding on tight to his sweat-slicked body, she moved her hips to the steamy rhythm he led. The sensations that swept through Amara, filling her with more ecstasy with each thrust, couldn't be described, only felt. Unable to get enough of him, all she could do was let loose her loving just as hotly as he let his loose on her.

Across town, Terrence lay in bed fantasizing as well. He relived the ecstasy he once experienced with Amara. He inhaled the sexy, fruity fragrance she loved to wear. He imagined his nose buried against her skin, drinking it in, and his lips tasting it.

Terrence imagined that he mingled his fingers in her long, flowing hair as well as the bushy hairs down below. He imagined stroking her breasts and easing his fingers below to the hairs above her vagina. He imagined slipping his fingers down farther and inside of her. After he had played with her enough, working her up until she begged him for his love, then they would truly enjoy each other.

Terrence would position himself on top of her, open her legs far apart and melt inside of Amara. His penis grew steel-like as he created it all in his mind. Terrence wanted to feel Amara's soaking, tight walls closing in all around him at that moment. However, the phone's harsh ring awakened him from his heated fantasy, and he picked up the receiver.

"Hello," he said breathily and wiped away perspiration beads that dampened his face.

"It's me," a deep voice responded.

Terrence perked up from his sensual haze and sat up. Richard Hayes, a friend, and the medical director of the mental facility where Michelle stayed wouldn't be calling at the late hour unless something had happened. "What has she done?"

"She almost got away."

Terrence felt the blood rise to his head. "How the hell did you let that happen?"

"I have to go home sometimes. She didn't escape on my watch!"

"That can't happen again!" Terrence stood from his clammy, silk sheets and paced. "Tell me the details."

"When we caught her, she was a good distance from the grounds. She claims she told someone what we were doing. Then, she said if I let her go, she would tell them that she lied. "

"That witch!" Terrence slammed his free hand into the wall.

"Do you think she's bluffing? Or did she tell someone what she's accusing us of?"

Speculating, Terrence didn't answer right away, and then finally said, "Keep her in line until I get there. I'll get a flight out tomorrow."

Chapter Nine

If only he had knew, what she had fantasized about him last night. Amara was constantly thinking this when she saw Bryce the next day at work. Easily she hid her secret desire among the day's general hustle and bustle. Saturday was the busiest day for a real estate agent, since many home seekers did their home searches on weekends.

This particular Saturday turned out to be more hectic than usual for Amara. If she wasn't out showing homes, she did listing presentations or followed up on loan applications. In addition, agreements needed party signatures, forms needed filling out, and calls needed to be made.

Since Terrence had flown out of town to check on his wife, Bryce took on the majority of his work. When he asked Amara if she could work late to assist him because his secretary had to be home with her family, she was thrilled with the idea.

Alone in the office, they worked together perfectly. Whether collaborating on the web content for a listing, or assessing a new property's value, they accomplished a great deal. They did it despite the sexual tension Amara sensed building between them. This tension oozed in every look Bryce gave her, in every casual touch, in the tone of his voice when he spoke to her, and in their every interaction. At one point when Amara became exhausted from all the hours of work, she even hated to go home. She wanted to savor every moment she had alone with Bryce and let her eyes devour this man who enchanted her.

"You mind if I stretch out on your couch for a bit?" she asked.

Bryce's dark eyes moved over her body swiftly and hungrily.

"Not at all. Relax and kick back."

"Thanks."

Amara lay down on the couch, and closed her eyes for several seconds, savoring their moment together. Opening her eyes, she saw Bryce watching her. He stopped instantly and switched his concentration to a document he worked on. She guessed the document had something to do with a multi-million dollar deal.

Amara admired him quietly. He was a genius, as Terrence had pointed out. More than that, he was a good man. His statements about his wife still intrigued and puzzled her.

"How did your wife pass away, if you don't mind my asking?" she threw into the quiet of the room.

Bryce rubbed his eyes as he looked up from the paperwork. "You mean Kim?"

"Yes."

"She had a weak heart since she was a child. We were childhood friends and we used to play together."

"Is that when you fell in love with her?"

He looked off smiling, as if recalling unforgettable memories. "I guess I did. We lived on the same block and were always hanging out together. She could be a tomboy at times, I mean as much as that heart of hers would let her."

"When did your relationship become more than friends?"

"When I learned she didn't have much more time on this earth."

"What do you mean?" Amara asked intently.

"We were always platonic friends. Then one day she told me how much she loved me, loved me in a romantic way. She said she dreamed of marrying me. She said she dreamed of it coming true, and she was the princess in a fairytale. So I made her dream come true. I didn't realize how much she made my fairytale come true too until she died. I truly did love her."

Amara eyed him with amazement. "You're a better man than I thought. It's a great thing you did. But you do so many great things. I heard around the office that you have some charitable and community projects lined up for the Porter Condominiums."

"I'm really excited about that."

"I'm excited for you. But I really find it so beautiful that you take the time to mentor young boys, too. Most men could care less."

"Hey, we have to be there for our little brothers who have been lacking in the dad department. If my dad wasn't there, who knows where I would be today."

Amara locked eyes with Bryce. Anyone could see that he was beautiful to look at, but it was his beautiful spirit as well that she found herself drawn to more and more. "You're something else."

"So are you. Look what you're doing for your brother."

"I love him. I can't help it. I can't stop wanting to help him."

"I can't stop wanting myself these days."

"Wanting what?" she asked, hoping that he would say he wanted her.

"Things that I shouldn't want." His eyes locked with hers so heatedly that Amara's heart raced. It raced far more when Bryce got up from his desk and walked to the sofa she lay on. "You look tired."

She smiled. "I had hoped it didn't show."

"Why don't you let me do something to help you relax and make you feel good?" he asked, his eyes swiftly roaming over her body. "Then I'll take you home."

Amara's heart felt like it stopped. "Like what?"

Bryce knelt down and brought his face near hers. "Let me give you a massage."

"A massage?" Her heart raged again. "You must be good."

"I'm real good."

In response, Amara granted him a closed-mouth smile and rolled on her stomach. Immediately Bryce's hands went to work. He massaged her shoulders deliciously, making her eyes flutter close. Soft moans escaped her as his large fingers worked magic on her sore arm muscles, and then he sensually moved his fingers back to her shoulders. With his every touch, desire grew within her, and her vagina began to throb with need.

Amara wanted him to pamper her back longer. It felt tight from her stress. However, her stiff, cotton blouse constricted him, keeping him from really rubbing her in the areas she needed. With her insides now wet, and aching for him stroke every inch of her, Amara turned around to face him. Bryce couldn't do much more with her top fitted so closely to her.

"I guess that's all you can do," she said, trying not to show how much he set her on fire. God knows she wanted so much more. "Thank you. That was wonderful."

Bryce's eyes ran the length of her body. "I can do more...if you just take off your blouse."

Amara stared up in his eyes, turned on by his smoldering stare. She nodded at his request, slowly unbuttoned her blouse, and gently tugged it off, revealing her lacy pink bra. For a long while, Bryce stared down at her hungrily, his chest heaving. When Amara rolled around on her stomach to feel his sensual massage, he snapped out of his trance.

His skillful fingers kneaded into her flesh until she felt him easing her around to face him. Lust drugged his already seductive eyes. His chest heaved even more. She knew he wanted her. Wanting him just as much, a pulsing sensation hit within the midst of her. Amara ached for him to soothe it.

She began to close in on his lips, but the phone's loud ring startled her. Bryce glanced at the clock and eyed the ringing phone almost angrily.

"Terrence and I scheduled a conference call for now."

Amara sat up and put her blouse back on. "You'd better answer it, then."

"Do you really want me to?" He held her gaze.

She stared in his eyes, so tempted to tell him not to answer it. However, there were serious reasons why they couldn't continue. "It doesn't matter what I want. It's what I need. I need to keep this job to help my brother and myself. And you need to keep your relationship and business straight with Terrence."

The phone rang again.

"We didn't do anything wrong, Amara. All I did was give you a massage."

"Do you think Terrence would have been okay with that if he walked in on us? Would he tell you that it's fine for you to put your hands on my body?"

Bryce hesitated answering. The phone continued to ring.

Amara stood and shuffled to the door. "I'll see you on Monday."

"Don't go. Please."

She gazed at him for a long while. "I have to."

Amara hurried out the door. She soon heard Bryce and Terrence on the speakerphone, having their conference call. Dazedly, she left the office and walked to her car in TJ Realty's parking lot. Confusion swirled in her head. She had attempted to explain to Bryce one of the reasons why she had to leave. Yet she had withheld another reason.

She could have thrown caution to the wind and dared to discover where that massage would have led them. She could have even convinced herself that if Terrence found out about their sizzling hot attraction and tried to destroy her again because she didn't want him, Bryce wouldn't have allowed him. Bryce would have ensured that she kept her job and position, or assisted her financially so that she would never have to worry. But, she knew better. Life had taught her that the one person she could count on was herself—Amara Hart.

Many miles away, Michelle Johnson didn't feel as tired as she normally did. Instead, fear consumed her. After hitting Nurse Henderson over the head with a soda bottle and failing in her attempt to escape, the medical director contacted her husband. Terrence was now on his way to the North Carolina mental health facility. She wondered what he planned to do to her.

Rocking back and forth on her bed, her mind traveled back nine years when her life had been so drastically different. Michelle, only child of one of the most successful real estate developers in the country, believed her life would always be blissful. Despite her mother's death from an aneurysm when she was an infant, her father provided her a dreamy existence, complete with the best of everything the world and money had to offer. She'd attended debutante balls, whimsical vacations in Paris, luxury custom made cars for her birthdays, credit cards with no limits, and her choice of the most desirable bachelors in the country.

Michelle never let anyone get in the way of what she wanted. So when she attended an annual real estate convention in Las Vegas with her father, and met Terrence Johnson, it didn't matter that the gorgeous entrepreneur accompanied his pregnant fiancé. It didn't matter that their wedding was two weeks away. When given the opportunity, Michelle lured him away to her hotel suite and seduced him for a weekend. Once he left her room, he returned to his fiancé and told her the wedding was off. The betrayed woman miscarried twin boys three days later. Michelle felt bad about the babies, but felt victorious taking away another woman's man.

A year and a half later, Michelle Hayworth became Michelle Hayworth Johnson. All would have been perfect if it weren't for her father's constant meddling in their marriage. Since the beginning of their courtship, her father disliked Terrence because he wasn't his daughter's equal financially and socially. As he came to know Terrence and the type of man he was, Evan Hayworth liked him even less. He distrusted Terrence so much he forbade his daughter to marry him, unless he signed an ironclad prenuptial agreement. Terrence eagerly signed and more love dust glistened from Michelle's eyes. She was blind. If only she had known then that her husband was an Oscar-worthy actor.

Still rocking back and forth on her bed, Michelle pushed aside her thoughts when her door opened. Though she had known Terrence was on his way to see her, it didn't prepare her when he stepped inside carrying roses. Just the sight of him enraged her.

"Hello, darling," Terrence greeted her.

"I am not your darling. You know that as well as I do."

Terrence grinned, closed the door, and walked toward his wife. He extended her the roses. "These are for you."

Michelle accepted the bouquet, and then tossed them across the room.

Terrence was amused. "Not your favorite flower I guess."

"I want to get out of here!"

"Sorry, dear. You need help."

"I sure do. That's why I got word to someone to help me when

I escaped. You're going to be in so much trouble; you're going to wish you were dead."

The smile vanished from Terrence's face. "How could I be in trouble for getting help for my very disturbed wife?"

"You liar! I am not crazy—but you are!"

As the summer heated up, so did Bryce's emotions for Amara. With each new day spent around her, he discovered more and more to admire about her. She was warm, intelligent, funny, caring and a super talented agent. During each moment he was in her company, he easily saw why Terrence had fallen under her seductive spell. She was a dream, in every way.

Throughout the passing, sizzling days, Bryce made an effort to avoid sensual encounters with her. Still, it did nothing to stop him from fantasizing about her and wanting her so badly that it hurt at times. What made it all the more unbearable was the sexual tension he felt building between them. He could look in Amara eyes and she would return a stare that, somehow silently, told how much she desired him.

One evening while they worked alone in the office, she conveyed this impassioned message more than ever before. Terrence was away on a business trip. Bryce's workload had piled up with his partner's work, too. He greatly needed an assistant. It was the first time Amara and he had been alone in the office since their last close call. He set up a workspace for her across the room while he sat behind his desk. He didn't want to make Amara feel like he planned to hit on her.

"So how is your brother?" he asked, watching her peck intently at computer keys.

Amara looked up from the keyboard. "I went to see him last week. He's making great progress. He might come home one of these days.'

"That's fantastic. I'd like to meet him…I mean if you don't mind."

Her full lips swirled up into a sensuous smile. "I don't mind at all."

"Good." He forced his interest back to his work, but felt her gaze on him. He looked back up and found Amara's luminous brown eyes staring at him. "Is everything okay?"

"Yes, I was just thinking about the last time I was here alone with you."

Bryce's heart beat a little faster at the memory of what could have been between them. "I was thinking about it, too."

Amara focused back on the computer, but then turned toward him again. "I always think about it."

Bryce swallowed as excitement rose up in him. Just hearing her say those words felt like the most beautiful gift. "So do I. I always think about you."

"You do? What do you think about?"

"That I can see why Terrence lost his mind over you." He swallowed again. "You're something else, Amara."

"I observe you every day. You're something else, too."

His gaze traveled the length of her body boldly. "I always wonder about that portrait you offered, too."

"What about it?"

"I never had the chance to finish the one in class, only got as far as your forehead. So, I'm always wondering about sketching you and painting you fully, so I can always see how beautiful you are."

Blushing, Amara lowered her head.

Bryce walked out from behind his desk. "Don't be shy about it. You are beautiful." He kneeled and Amara swiveled her chair so that he was in front of her. "I didn't think you were kidding when you told me you would pose for me again."

Warmly she gazed into his eyes. "You were right. I wanted to do it for you."

"Do you still want to?" His voice lowered to a near whisper and the erection that took hold of him the instant they were alone together made him feel even more aroused.

"Yes," Amara answered softly.

"Do you still want to do that for me?" His heart froze awaiting her answer.

"Yes."

His finger glided along her arm. "Can we start now?"

"Now? Here?"

Bryce saw how his touch affected her, making her bite her lip. "Yes, I want to sketch you. There's no one here but us." His fingers moved up to her shoulder.

"What about all the work that needs to be done now?"

"I want to go with the flow of this moment." He gazed in her eyes as his finger approached her neckline. "Because it just feels so damn exciting. I know you feel it too."

"I do."

Bryce felt her trembling and grew more titillated. "So can we do it?"

Slowly, Amara nodded. "All right."

Bryce was so thrilled that he didn't know what to do first, get the pad and pen, or get Amara on the couch. Deciding on the latter, Bryce escorted Amara to the black, leather sofa. Easily, she sprawled sideways in an ultra sexy pose, while seemingly whispering to him with her eyes that she was his in any way he desired her.

Swallowing the rush in his throat the excitement caused, Bryce kneeled again and touched the top button of her blouse. He followed to the next button and the next, until her blouse stood open. He noticed that her red satin bra unhooked from the front. She gave him a look that granted him permission to reveal her. And he did, removing the blouse and the bra. Clad only in her short skirt, stockings and heels, Amara took his breath away.

"Jesus," Bryce said looking down at her succulent breasts. "I don't even think I can sketch you. You make me so hot."

"Do you want to touch me, Bryce?"

"I want to do more than touch you," he answered, feeling an erection that made him ache for her. "I want to kiss you all over. And I'll start with this."

Breath caught in his throat as she guided his hands over her soft, large breasts. At the same time, his mouth pressed hers and his tongue explored the honey between her lips. He felt Amara clasping her arms around his wide shoulders. It felt heavenly and he craved her to hold him as tightly as she could.

Bryce drew her deeper into him. He grew drugged from the delicious, strawberry- based fragrance she wore. Combined with the erotic excitement she whipped up within his body, his penis grew even more concrete hard. He was so aroused by kissing her, he knew he was about to burst if he didn't have her. Swirling his tongue around hers, he became addicted to her taste. Gliding his mouth downward, he couldn't get enough of kissing, sucking and licking her breasts. Her lush nipples felt like smooth round marbles. His moans and her whimpers blended like a sensual groove, as they whipped each other into an erotic frenzy.

Though, just as he began to ease her back down on the couch with his body, the door flung open. Shocked someone had remained in the office and caught them, Amara pushed Bryce off of her and grabbed her top. Trying to catch his breath, Bryce sprang to his feet.

Chapter Ten

Relief washed over Bryce when he saw that it wasn't Terrence unexpectedly returning early from his business trip. It wasn't a relief, however, to see the intruder was one of his real estate agents. Elaine Reardon looked as embarrassed as they did with shock spread all over her face. Bryce felt his entire body clench.

"I left my house keys on my desk and came back to get them," she explained. "I thought I heard a prowler in here. I didn't know anyone was staying late tonight. I parked in front of the building instead of the lot, so I didn't see your cars there."

"It's okay. And we just had some things to take care of," Bryce informed her.

With her small eyes blinking rapidly, Elaine looked from Amara to Bryce. "I'm sorry to interrupt."

Amara offered her a closed-lipped smile as she finished buttoning her blouse. "It's all right."

Backing away, she hurried out of the office. "See you."

The instant Elaine closed the door, Bryce felt his tightened muscles relax. "Let's go to my place."

Wildly Amara shook her head. "No."

"We can be alone there and don't have to worry about who is going to walk in on us."

"Bryce, we can't do this."

"Amara, I know you were going crazy like I was. I know you were feeling that insatiable heat just as I was. I know it."

"Yes, I was. And believe me, I wanted even more. But we were caught. Do you know what that means?" She began to pace and her gaze scattered over the room frantically. "She could tell her friends and it will ultimately get back to Terrence."

"Maybe he should find out." He didn't want to hide what he felt for her.

"No."

"Yes. Why can't we tell him we're extremely attracted to each other? He'll just have to get over it."

Amara's eyes widened with astonishment. "Are you talking about Terrence Johnson, the one who destroyed me, who caused me to lose job after job?"

Bryce's brows puckered with confusion. "What are you talking about?"

"I'm talking about how Terrence tried to ruin my life after I left here. Each time I got hired at top real estate firms, like Henderson and Wentworth, he bought them out. And each time, I was let go because he had other staff in place."

Bryce's head spun with this news. "I had no idea he did that." Frowning, he shook his head. "I had no idea."

"You know now."

"I knew he was crazy jealous, but that was too much." Speechless, he looked off thinking, and then gazed back at her. "Let's think about us for now. There is something between us. You feel it just as I do. We can't deny it anymore. Let's see where this takes us."

Amara frowned. "I really want to, Bryce, but..."

"Then please come home with me," he pleaded with her.

"Why don't you let me think about it? I mean about coming home with you another time. Elaine seeing us like that really scares me."

Moments later, Amara started up her car and drove until she couldn't drive any more. She parked downtown, hoping the bright lights that lit up the avenue would distract her from what bothered her. It did no good. She saw only what was in her mind. God knows kissing Bryce and having him touch her the way he did, made her ache for so much more that it actually hurt.

On the other hand, how could she entertain the idea of having more of him when someone from the firm had seen them getting intimate, especially when that someone's mouth had the power to destroy her world again? Amara didn't know what to do. Should she go with her feelings, or try to stay away from a man who made her feel more alive and womanly than she had felt in a long time? She didn't know how much she had missed a man's touch until she felt the hunger of Bryce's kiss on her lips and body. His touch made her feel desired.

Amara entered Jamie's house that night, looking forward to a girl chat with her sensible friend. She knew Jamie would applaud how far Bryce and she had gone tonight. Her friend would grant her blessing about Bryce. First, she needed to freshen up. Quietly she ascended the stairs, and strolled down the thickly carpeted hallway to her room. Unexpectedly, Carlyn stepped out of Jamie's room.

"Wow, you're home late," she remarked.

Amara sighed. "There was a lot to do at the office. I'm bushed."

"I bet. I bet it was hot up in there."

Amara scowled at the comment. "Why do you say that?"

"Because the temperature was so crazy hot today that there were power outages in that area."

"Fortunately, there wasn't one in our office."

"Good. Well, take care."

Amara studied Carlyn as she strode down the hall humming. Could she have known her secret already? She had seen Elaine talking to her a few times when they all had worked together. Then again, maybe she was being paranoid.

Once she showered, relaxed, and ate dinner, Amara and Jamie chilled out on the porch swing. Jamie seemed thrilled about Amara and Bryce getting more intimate. If only they hadn't been caught, Amara would have felt wonderful about it too.

"I don't think I can resist him anymore," she shared. "Not after tonight."

Jamie patted her hand. "Do what your heart is telling you. Enjoy the ride. Falling in love is one of the best thing things there is."

Amara eyed her amusedly. "Who said I was in love?"

"You don't have to say it. Girl, it's all over you."

"But I still feel like I don't know everything about him. Sometimes, I'm scared he's going to change and show me a dark side, like Terrence did. How could I possibly be falling in love?"

"Love is love. We don't know why we feel it for someone. God just puts it in our hearts and it's there. And girl, it's not going away."

Seated in a limousine that whisked him from the airport to his home, Terrence checked the numerous messages at his home phone, his cellular, and then his office. He looked bewildered when he heard an annoying voice from the past.

"Terrence, this is Carlyn Chandler. I hope you haven't forgotten me. I'm the pretty, slender agent with a big afro and big, hazel eyes who worked for you a few years ago. I need to talk to you about something. It's real important. You really need to hear what I have to tell you. Could you please give me a call?"

Carlyn went on to recite her home, cellular and office numbers. Terrence didn't bother to jot them down. Nothing she had to say would interest him. When she worked for him, she struck him as a lazy, little gold digger. She was the first to go when he downsized because she made too many personal calls, didn't interact well with clients, and rarely sold a house. Worst of all, she asked him for money several times and threw her body at him, every chance she could—a body that made him soft instead of hard. Carlyn was not his cup of tea. He didn't even want to give her a sympathy screw. Hence, he deleted her message.

Over the next week, Amara saw little of Bryce, because their schedules became so hectic. He had a myriad of meetings, while Amara's success with selling homes flourished. Sales of some of the most sumptuous mansions in Maryland stacked up in her portfolio. When Terrence pressed her about going to lunch with him to celebrate her victories, she agreed. After all, she had dined with Bryce in the past to celebrate her sales achievements. Terrence might have become

Kiss Me All Over

suspicious, if she didn't indulge him with the same consideration.

High, domed bright ceilings and huge chandeliers graced the Ritz Maynard hotel's elegant dining room where Amara and Terrence dined. The twosome feasted on bacon-wrapped scallops, Caesar salad, herb-creamed fettucine, roasted glazed eggplant, buttermilk shrimp, barbecued lobster, crab-stuffed filets, honeyed potatoes, and sesame seared tomatoes. While they enjoyed the meal, they shared stories about some of the kooky clients who wandered through TJ Realty's doors from time to time. As Amara bent over, laughing hard, she had almost forgotten the sense of humor Terrence always possessed. It was a surprisingly pleasant lunch date. Until, that is, he reached across the table and stroked her hand. As Terrence did this, his humored expression transformed into an intense one.

"This is almost like old times," he said.

"Almost." The joy drained from Amara's face and she threw Terrence a cautious look. She didn't want to deal with any drama and prayed that he would back off.

"Girl, I love you and I miss you."

Amara eased her hand back from his. "Terrence I thought you weren't going to do this."

"I can't help myself. I love you, Amara."

"Stop staying that," she said, wishing it was someone else professing those words.

"But I do love you."

"What about your wife?"

"We're in the final stages of our divorce."

Wildly, Amara shook her head. "Don't do this."

"We can make it work, Amara." His chest heaved as he spoke. "We can start right now by going upstairs to one of those suites and do what we used to do so well."

"Oh, so that's why you brought me to a hotel restaurant?" she asked, wishing it was Bryce who had brought her here and made such a proposal. "It's not happening!"

"Can I help that I want you so badly? It was never that hot with any other woman."

"Stop, Terrence." Now, she knew he couldn't handle her with

84

Bryce. "Just stop!"

"It's true.

"Please stop!" Amara demanded.

"All right, I will if you don't want anything to do with me that way. Fine, I'd rather be a friend in your life than not have you in my life at all."

To that, Amara eyed him suspiciously.

Amara thought of Terrence's words after she returned to the office and carried on with her day. If only he was sincere about their friendship being just friendship. Yet she knew Terrence Johnson, and knew better. He would continue to try to lure her into his bed. It made it all more complicated to feel what she did for Bryce. She couldn't bear to think about what Terrence would do if he had any clue that she desired someone close to him—his best friend. He would become the devil himself if he knew that she and Bryce ached for each other. The more Terrence wanted her, the more it seemed she wanted Bryce.

Amara hung around the office that evening because she knew Terrence had a dinner meeting across town. Bryce remained alone. When she walked into his office, he sat behind the desk. He looked happy and surprised to see her.

Mysteriously silent, she strolled over to him and couldn't resist holding his face. His skin was smooth and smelled like aftershave. Bryce stood, put his arms around her, and crushed his soft mouth against hers. Her insides were set on fire. As she enjoyed the luscious taste of his lips and tongue, she felt his body harden against her. The sound of distant whistling distracted them. They pulled apart just as Terrence opened the door to Bryce's office.

Chapter Eleven

Terrence stopped in his tracks, eyeing them both, curiously. "Is there a party going on in here?" He laughed as he spoke, but Amara noted his eyes didn't match the comment.

Bryce grinned. "Just burning the midnight oil."

"Both of you?"

Amara stepped toward the office door. "I was just asking my boss if I could help with anything before I left."

Terrence nodded, but still looked stumped by the awkwardness of the scene.

"How was the business dinner?" Bryce sat on the edge of his desk and folded his arms. "How did we make out?"

"Prosperously." Terrence touted.

"All right!" Bryce raised his fist in victory. "You need to fill me in on all the details."

"I will," Terrence said, his gold-brown eyes shifting back to Amara. "So you're headed home now?"

"I sure am, I'm leaving now. See you guys on Monday. Have a great weekend."

Outside, Amara's heels clacked against the concrete of TJ Realty's parking lot. All the while, she wondered if Bryce and she had moved apart fast enough. Had Terrence seen something? He seemed dazed by the sight of them together. Then again, perhaps he just didn't expect them to work so late in the office together.

Scooting down on the seat of her car, Amara wondered what was she going to do. Clearly, she couldn't stay away from Bryce. She couldn't stop thinking of him. She couldn't stop wanting him. And more than ever, she was convinced that it felt so right between them because it was right. Bryce was a good man, who made her feel safe, protected, and even though he never said it, loved.

She wondered what time he planned to leave the office. After that last smoldering kiss, she ached for him like never before. When he went home tonight, she planned to be there, too. She had to make love with Bryce tonight.

Inside the office, Bryce noticed that Terrence looked and behaved a bit mystified. Bryce was certain he hadn't seen them kissing. Yet, he wondered if Terrence had picked up the vibes that Amara and he desired each other. Several times, he started to confess, but stopped before the words left his mouth. He checked himself when he thought of Amara. He couldn't tell Terrence about them until she was more comfortable with their relationship.

Bryce listened to Terrence sharing the details of his successful business meeting. At one point, Terrence's words blurred beneath his thoughts. Sensual images had taken over—images of kissing every inch of Amara's naked body.

The fantasies persisted after Bryce left TJ Realty, put gas in his car, and stopped by his local grocer for his beloved famous Amos Cookies. While driving down the dark empty highway, he knew he would have to call Amara, tonight. She probably felt shaken up about Terrence walking in. He wanted to soothe her worries. But more than that, he had to tell her what he felt. He had to show her what he felt. He had to make love to her.

Steering his silver, Mercedes-Benz on his S driveway, Bryce spotted Amara's car parked on his estate and his heart did a leap. He parked and she raced over to him.

"Make love to me tonight?" she whispered.

"Making love to you is all I can think about."

Inside the house, Amara couldn't wait for Bryce to take her upstairs to his bed. She eased down on the living room couch. Bryce got on his knees in front of her. Her eyes riveted to his tasty looking lips. Amara slanted toward him. But before she had the chance to kiss him first, Bryce thrust his tongue inside her mouth. She couldn't get enough of tasting his raw, seductive flavor. Red-hot tremors raced through her. Before long, she felt him pulling her down on the floor with him. She was pleasantly pinned beneath him.

Once body to body, his rock hardness prodded into her. Amara lost herself in the feeling of his excitement and wrapped her arms around his back. At the same time, Bryce swirled his tongue erotically around hers. Drinking up his love juices and holding him, she weakened to an unbearable point.

Suddenly Bryce rose up off her, hurried out of his shirt, and began unbuttoning her blouse.

Amara stared up at him whimpering, "I need to feel you, now."

"Oh, baby, all I've been dreaming about is feeling you. I'm going to go so deeply inside of you."

After tossing her blouse aside, Bryce unhooked her front-closure red bra, and buried his face against her chest. The silky wetness of his mouth on her breasts had Amara shivering. Her nipples grew to marble hard peaks as his tongue flicked across them. Whipping her into even more of a sexual frenzy, his hands dipped down into her pants, stimulating her, caressing precisely above her warm, moist place.

Having titillated her enough, Bryce unzipped her pants and within a breath, stripped her of everything. As she remained on the floor, naked before him, he stared at her and tore off his own clothes. Bare and naked, he looked so sexy she ached with need just imagining him inside of her. But soon he allayed the sweet torture, dipping his head past her waist.

Amara's hips flung upward as his tongue's velvetiness pleased her wet, tight honey. Her loud moans and screams filled the air. At times, she hardly recognized her own voice. Swept up in the erotic sensations, she swore nothing could feel any more luscious. When she believed the pleasure had reached its peak, he treated her to a new level of arousal, sucking her clitoris, teasing it with his tongue, and stimulating it with both his lips and fingers. Quivering from the ecstasy exploding through her body, she never wanted the moment to end.

Amara was soaking wet and her vagina throbbing for him by

the time she had the pleasure of stuffing his super long penis into a condom. Soon after, his nude wet body melded with hers. Amara's heart pound fiercely, savoring his bare flesh against hers. He reached beneath her, firmly palming her buttocks. When he hoisted his hips and reached down low between their bodies, her heartbeat seemed to freeze. Bryce's fingers slid in and out of her wet warmth, hitting her spot again, driving her crazy before he spread her legs far apart.

Just the tip of him drove of her wild. Bit by bit, he pushed letting her enjoy every inch of him that filled her. Then, at last, sweeter than any dreamed she dreamed about him, he moved in and out, pleasuring her with rapture unlike any she had ever known.

As their love grew so hot she could barely stand it, Bryce pinned her arms above her head and held her still as she lost control and thrashed beneath him. But Amara knew she couldn't hold on to paradise forever. The ultimate joy gripped her. As Bryce's muscles contracted violently and he lapped up the juices from her mouth as if starved, she knew he felt the same.

Motionless, Terrence sat in a brown, leather lumbar chair in his office, wishing he didn't feel the emptiness he did. He couldn't even celebrate the triumph of his meeting because of it—because he smelled something nasty. Had Bryce and Amara made a fool of him? His heart raced from the instant he walked in the office, and it hadn't slowed yet.

No, he hadn't witnessed them engaging in anything out of the ordinary. Despite that, their faces and body language made the hairs on the back of his neck stand up. Somehow, they looked different. They reminded him of kids who had been caught sneaking candy from someone who wasn't supposed to see. Something wasn't right.

On the other hand, was his insecurity getting the best of him? After all, he longed for Amara to dance dirty with him on his silken bed sheets more than anything on this earth. She expressed that her heart wasn't in the same place. Was it that he couldn't even stand to see her talking with his best friend, or being around him? But Bryce was more than a best friend. He was his brother, in every way. They had never wandered that dangerous territory of trying to get with each other's woman. It was an unstated oath between them.

Attempting to shake off the sick feelings, Terrence checked his messages. First, he listened to the ones at his home. Second, he jotted down numbers to call back from his cell phone's service. Lastly, he scribbled communications left at his office.

Hearing Carlyn's irritating voice again aggravated him. He cut off the machine. Though, after a moment of speculation, his curiosity was piqued. Why was she so desperate to speak with him? He pressed the play button to hear her full recording.

"Terrence, this is Carlyn, the cute one, remember? You never returned my phone call. Please call me. Elaine, one of your agents, is my buddy. She keeps me updated on what's happening at your company. She told me something about your partner, Bryce, and Amara. I think you should know about."

Nearly an hour later, Terrence had not only phoned Carlyn, but now sat across from her at the eatery she dubbed her favorite, Red Lobster. Having no appetite after hearing her message, he let her help herself to the shrimp, lobster, clams, salad, fries, punch, and cheddar biscuits garnishing their table. Endlessly she chattered about her new position, outfits she wanted to purchase at a new, ritzy boutique, and how hard it was to find a good man. Having finally heard enough of her endless chatter, Terrence waved his hand for her to hush.

Scowl lines marred her narrow face. "What's the matter?"

"Nothing is the matter. I just didn't come here to hear all this."

"You invited me to dinner."

"So you could tell me about what you know of Amara and Bryce."

"I'm going to tell you."

"When?"

"Why are you so rush, rush with me?" She bit a biscuit and chewed as she talked. "We haven't seen each other in such a long time. Can't you take a minute to get reacquainted?"

"Look, woman, my time is precious."

Carlyn reared back, stunned. "My time is precious, too. Lots of guys would be glad to be here with me."

"So where the hell are they?" he asked testily.

Carlyn drew back farther at his tone. "What are you mad at me for? Don't take it out on me. I'm not the one who backstabbed you. Maybe I should keep my secret about your buddy and Amara all to myself. What do you think about that?"

Terrence regretted losing his composure. He knew he had to make an effort to tone down his frustration and act less impatient if he wanted to get the information he wanted to confirm what his gut instinct had already screeched at him.

"I'm sorry," he apologized, dabbing at his temple. "I'm just beginning to sense something between them and it's getting to me."

"Hey, I can understand that." She dabbed at her cleavage, revealed in her low cut blouse. "I have a little itch here." She smiled seductively.

Terrence returned a plastic smile. "So what is it?" He leaned forward, his stomach clenching, as he braced himself. "What is going on between them?"

Carlyn threw her hand up. "Baby, hold up. Hold up. Relax and wait a minute. In fact, why don't we go back to your place and I can tell you privately?"

"You can tell me here! This has dragged on long enough. You had me come here to tell me something."

"But you didn't answer my question."

"About what?" He gnashed his teeth.

"About us getting busy at your place." She thrust her chest forward to give him a better view. "I heard you have a real nice mansion. Why don't you show it to me?"

"Because I don't have time."

"You have time for her." She licked her lips.

Terrence hid how sickened she made him. "Who?"

"Amara, that's who! And she doesn't even deserve it."

"Look, are you going to tell me or not?" Terrence was so annoyed that he couldn't even pretend to like her.

"Are we going to go back to your place, or not? I can't believe you're not hyped up about getting some of this?" Her hand swept along her lanky body.

"I'd rather give you money than do that." He reached in his back pocket for his wallet.

Carlyn stood before he could take anything out. Her hazel eyes thinned as if they were slits. "Don't be so insulting!"

"I'm sorry. But since when did the offer of money insult you?"

"You would rather pay me than sleep with me?"

"I'm tired, okay?"

"Yeah, right. You wouldn't be too tired to hump Amara's big butt. But unfortunately, for you, your best friend is already doing that. I guess she likes his stuff better. He looks like he's a much bigger man, if you know what I mean."

Mixing a smirk with her fury, Carlyn flounced around and strutted away from his table. Terrence was tempted to grab her and shake her for her dig at him. However, he needed to keep his cool and focus his rage elsewhere. They would be sorry, soon enough.

Chapter Twelve

Bryce continued to thrill Amara with spicy, hot love. Whether on her stomach, her knees, on top of him, against the wall, draped over the corners of the sofa, he loved her in a variety of positions and in various rooms throughout his mansion. Exhausted to the point of passing out, Amara couldn't go on any longer. In his bed, she snuggled against Bryce's sticky body, until they both dozed off.

Waking up together, her nude buttocks brushed the front of him. He hardened so much he had to have her again. Soon, she felt him clamp her hips while he unleashed his sweet whip on her from the back. As he moved his hardness against her, while sprinkling kisses on the back of her shoulders, she swore she heard something. She cocked her ear toward where she heard the thump in the distant background. Hearing nothing, she let herself enjoy Bryce's seduction again. But then she heard it again.

Amara convinced Bryce to investigate. Reluctantly, he did. When he returned, he put her at ease. He had forgotten to lock up with the alarm. However, the home was undisturbed. There hadn't been an intruder.

Before long, Amara lay on his chest, amazed that they had actually made love. Bryce kissed her forehead while his fingertips drew soft sensual circles on her belly.

"How long did you want to get in my pants?" She curved her head upward to see his face when he answered.

Bryce grinned. "Now, why do you have to ask like that?"

"Answer the question, mister lover boy."

"I'm scared to."

Amara laughed. He laughed with her.

"All right, I won't lie. I wanted you ever since we worked together the first time. But that's not all I want. I'm feeling something I didn't plan on."

Amara knew exactly what he meant. "What?" She propped herself up and kissed him. As their lips separated, he shook his head at her.

"You. You're too much. You really rocked me."

Amara dropped her eyes to his massive chest and stroked it. "You know how to rock pretty well yourself. I can't get over how you made me feel." She gazed up into his eyes. "I can't get over that I'm here with you. It's as if we don't know everything about each other, but somehow we do know each other. Does that sound crazy?"

"Not at all. There is this strong connection that's always pulled us together. And after tonight I can bet it will only get stronger and deeper."

"I want to know everything about you, Bryce."

"Does that mean you're going to spend time with me?"

"You can see as much of me as you want."

"Umm." He leaned down and kissed her hungrily.

Since a beautiful Sunday awaited, Amara decided to spend the entire day with Bryce. To avoid running into Terrence, they headed three towns away to take in a movie and dinner. Afterward, they basked on the sunny shores of Ocean City and wrapped up their time making love in the car. Amara kept wondering if she dreamed every moment.

Humming as she entered Jamie's house that evening, Amara recalled that her friend worked on an Atlanta flight that night. It was too bad. Amara couldn't wait to tell Jamie what had happened with Bryce. She knew Jamie would be happy for her.

Strolling through the living room, hunger pains got the best of her. Surely, Bryce had fed her well throughout their day together. Still, she assumed all that hot lovemaking in the car during the evening had burned up her calories. Amara smiled, remembering the deliciously naughty things he did to her. But she lost her thoughts once she entered the kitchen. A bald, forty-something man sat at the table. Eating a sandwich, he surprised her.

"Hello," she said. "You must be a friend of Carlyn's.

"Yes, I am. I'm Phil." He extended his hand.

Amara felt a firm handshake. "It's nice to meet you, Phil. I'm Amara. Where's Carlyn?"

"Trying to get to her man before you jump his bones!" From the living room, Carlyn flitted in the kitchen, seething.

Amara half-smiled, half-frowned at her tirade. "Are you kidding?"

"Do I look like I'm kidding?"

"I was just being polite to your guest."

"By throwing your big rump in his face?"

The man's tiny eyes tripled in size. "No, Carlyn, it wasn't like that," he said.

"Don't tell me it wasn't! She's always after somebody's man, married men included. But now stuff has caught up to her and it's really going to hit the fan!"

Amara frowned at her. "What in the world are you talking about?"

"You'll see!" Carlyn grasped her friend's hand, yanked him up from the chair, and pulled him out of the kitchen.

Once alone, Amara replayed the scene in her head and not only grew baffled, but a bit frightened. Carlyn's statement had promised some drama. Had Elaine told her?

Bryce found the next week at work to be as hectic as it was incredible. Terrence and he joined forces with several entertainment entrepreneurs and closed the biggest deal of their lifetime. Magnificent as it was, it was also stressful for him to share such an achievement with Terrence when there was uncertainty about their future as partners and as friends. Surely, he had to tell Terrence about his recent involvement with Amara. From his perspective, Terrence had no right to be that angry anyway. Though, he claimed to be getting a divorce from Michelle, he was in fact, still married. Terrence was unavailable, but Bryce was not.

This week, however, was not the time for confessions. The deal of all deals had them party planning. They had such a coup, they planned a grand soirée on Terrence's estate. On the night of the big bash, he wanted to escort Amara. In light of their situation, he opted to meet her there instead. Eventually they intended to sneak off and be alone for a little while.

At Terrence's estate, Amara met a number of the music industry's hottest celebrities, ranging from singers and producers, to managers and publicists, along with other VIP's. The current business merger had been made with several entertainment executives, so she expected to see this type of crowd at the party. As she circled the room, overwhelmed with excitement, she searched for Bryce. Instead, Terrence came her way, looking debonair in a beige, custom-cut Italian suit. She could tell he had been drinking because his eyes were glassy. Shamelessly, his eyes roamed over the red, slinky dress she wore.

"Damn, baby, you look good tonight." Terrence clasped Amara's hand, and maneuvered her to get a good look at the front and back of the backless outfit.

The display made Amara uncomfortable, but she tried not to show it. "Thanks. This is a great party, Terrence."

"Isn't it?" Looking wild-eyed, Terrence quickly scanned the crowded room. "But it would be a better party upstairs. The Terrence and Amara party." He laughed.

Amara told herself it was the liquor talking and tried to change the subject. "Where are the rest of the TJ agents?"

"Around. Anyone special you're looking for?"

For a second, the question made her wonder if he knew about Bryce and her. What if Elaine had told Carlyn what she'd seen at the office? Then again, she was certain Carlyn's tirade had been about pure jealousy and insecurity. She shook off her fears. "I was just wondering where the rest of the staff is."

"Oh, you'll see them soon enough. But forget them. You didn't answer my question."

Amara spotted a colleague and had a legitimate excuse to

escape Terrence. Amara socialized with the loads of guests Terrence had invited to his party, while hoping Bryce would soon join her. When he finally rang her cell phone, she hurried on the terrace for privacy. Answering the call, she said in a low voice, "Hello, lover."

Bryce chuckled at the greeting, but at the same time, he sounded like something was wrong.

"Where are you?" she asked.

"I'm sorry, Amara. I'm going to have to miss the party tonight."

Her heart sank. "Why? It's your celebration. Your and Terrence's."

"I know, but it's the young man I mentor, Chris."

"What about him?"

"He had a bike accident," he said in a dejected tone.

"Oh, no."

"His mom called me just as I was about to leave for the party."

"Was he hurt badly?"

"He wasn't wearing his helmet and crashed into a fence. He has a big lump on his head. But they say the x-ray showed no damage, and he's talking up a storm, like always."

Amara sighed with relief. "Well, that's good."

"I think so too. They're going to keep him overnight for observation. So I'm going to stay at the hospital a while and go crash at home. I don't really feel like partying when my man here is hurt. I'll call Terrence and tell him the situation. I'm sure he won't be as understanding, though."

"Because he's not thoughtful and sweet like you."

"You really mean that?"

"Oh, yes." Amara replied.

"Then come by my house later after the party, and I'll show you how sweet I can be."

"I'll be there. I can't wait to be with you."

Moments after their call ended, Amara stood in the same spot thinking. Of course, she was terribly disappointed that Bryce couldn't celebrate his success and be with her. On other hand, what he was doing showed her even more what a wonderful person he was. She felt so blessed to have this man in her life.

As the evening continued, Amara tried to enjoy herself without Bryce. She danced, nibbled hors d'oeuveres, roamed the mansion's many rooms with her colleagues, explored the game room, and wandered out poolside where a woman stripped, to many men's delight. Wanting to hurry to Bryce's place, she caught up to Terrence to thank him for the evening. He looked sloshed.

"I think I'm going to go now," she told him.

Terrence blinked his bloodshot eyes. "Why?"

"Because I'm tired and sleepy."

"Is that the only reason?" He wobbled a bit.

"Yes, why else?"

"Just wondering. Just wondering if you're trying to find a way to get out of sleeping with me!" He spoke so loudly that Amara glimpsed around to see who heard him.

But she was tempted to yell too—yell about how he had ruined her life. Thank God for Bryce, she could move forward. "Terrence, don't start." Taking note of the people around them, she kept her voice low. "Please don't start."

"Don't start what? You used to give me all of that good stuff. Why can't I have some now? You here that everybody!" He was yelling. "I used to get all this good stuff and it is as good as it looks." Laughing heartily, he staggered away.

Amara didn't even bother to look around and see who heard the humiliating words. She hurried out the door and toward her car. Once inside it, she tried to just drive off and attempt to forget about him. Yet, her heart raced too fast. Her body trembled. With all that, she kept imagining how people laughed and talked about what he said. Terrence would never behave civilly toward her. She felt foolish to think she could work with him without any problems. She was even more foolish for trusting him after he had caused her to be homeless.

When Bryce opened the door, he expected to see Amara's sexy smile. Instead, it tore him apart to see her tears. Ushering her inside, he asked frantically, "What happened? Why are you crying?"

Amara leaned back against the foyer's wall as Bryce closed the door. "Your partner really did me in tonight. He was drinking and he was so awful."

Bryce wiped a tear that rolled down Amara's cheek and prayed that Terrence hadn't tried to take what he wanted. "He didn't…He didn't try to force you did he?"

Amara sniffled. "He said things about us going to bed. But that wasn't the bad part. What was so awful was his telling the entire party about our bedroom activities. About how I was in bed with him. It was so embarrassing." She broke into tears.

Hearing what Terrence did made such rage well up in Bryce that he wanted to unleash at that moment on Terrence. Yet, he could see how upset Amara was. She needed his comfort, more than Terrence needed his fist.

"I'll take care of him, baby," his voice rasped, just before he pressed his mouth against hers and pierced her lips apart with his tongue.

Amara's tongue swirled hungrily around his. His penis, which became hard just seeing her, hardened another rung. Bryce picked Amara up and her arms clung to him. Kissing away her every tear as it fell, he carried her upstairs to his bedroom.

There, Bryce sat on the side of the bed while Amara stood between his legs, undressing. When Amara was naked at last, he kissed her hairy patch. His hands glided along the sides of her hips and thighs while she rubbed his hair. Feeling like he was on fire, his hands wandered up to her breasts. Squeezing them, making himself aroused and seeing how aroused he made her, he became bolder. Letting his mouth wander deeper between her legs, he pleased her with pointed flicks of his tongue.

When Amara began to quiver and whimper, Bryce guided her down on his bed. He stood above her, gazing down at her body while removing his clothes. Once bare, he worked on a condom and joined her on the bed.

Bryce kissed her mouth, tasting her as if she were his last meal on earth. With every swirl of his tongue in her honey, his body welled up with hot-blooded desire. Tantalizing her with kisses, Bryce set out to do the same with his hands. They were all over her, especially her tight, wet place. He lingered there, penetrating her with his fingers, stimulating her with the motions of intercourse.

Then, after licking his fingers and hers, he decided to give her what they both hungered for. Positioning himself between her legs, he threw each of them over his shoulders. His thick penis soon pushed into her as far as it would go.

Amara's legs trembled, as they both became one, and she held onto to Bryce tightly. As he moved inside her, the pleasure made him crazed. As he moaned and she screamed, she swayed her hips spicily and held him deep within her wet walls. Thrusting her with erotic, circular movements and then with in and out grinds, Bryce held her legs in place over his shoulders. But all too soon, the strain of holding on to the rapture became too much. Their sweat-drenched bodies shuddered before they collapsed and lay still.

Hours later, Amara awakened and woke Bryce up with a kiss on his lips.

Drowsily, he gazed at her and smiled. "Beautiful woman, you put it on me again."

"You are so fresh, Bryce Davidson."

"And you love me that way, don't you?"

"Yes, I do love you," she whispered, and then searched his face for his response.

Bryce stared at her with a mixture of warmth and desire radiating in his eyes. "I love you, too." Softly he kissed her lips. "I can't believe how fast it happened, but I do."

Amara glowed from his touching words, but looked away sadly.

Clutching her cheeks, he guided her face back toward his. "I know what you're thinking. I'm going to straighten Terrence out about showing his butt tonight."

Amara shook her head. "Maybe it's best that we forget it."

"Amara, we can't forget it. Just like we can't hide what's happening with us. He has to know. I think he and I can work this out, if we talk about it."

"He'll be vengeful," she pointed out. "Believe me, I know. And what about your new venture?"

"What about it? It's about money. I have plenty of that, but I only have one of you."

He closed in on her lips and kissed them passionately. Only the ringing phone forced them apart. At such a late hour, Bryce thought it might have been about Chris.

He swiped up the phone. "Hello."

"Bryce? Bryce is that you?"

The woman's voice sounded vaguely familiar. She sounded muffled and far away.

"Yes, this is Bryce. Who is this?"

"It's Michelle, Terrence's wife."

Surprise widened his eyes. Bryce couldn't imagine why Michelle would call him. He didn't even know she had his number. "Michelle? How are you? Are you okay?"

"No. I need your help."

"My help?" He frowned as he tried to make sense of her contacting him. Why wouldn't she call her husband? "What's the matter? Where are you?"

"I'm still in this hell hole. Please help me."

"Hell hole?" He glanced at Amara, who watched and listened carefully. "What's going on? How can I help you?"

"You can save me from him." She sounded desperate.

"Him?"

"Terrence. He's trying to kill me."

Chapter Thirteen

Bryce listened to Michelle for several minutes before a bad connection ended their call. Repeatedly she stated that Terrence had tried to kill her. Bryce, having known Terrence for many years, assured her that couldn't have possibly been the case. He knew Terrence was no angel, especially after his behavior tonight with Amara. Still, he also knew he would never harm his wife, or God forbid, take her life.

"What if she's telling the truth?" Amara asked, nudging Bryce from the deep thoughts consuming him after the troubling call.

"Because I know him. Besides, she didn't even say why or how he was trying to do this. She just kept ranting that he was trying to kill her."

"How ill is she?"

"Well, Terrence said she's exhibited many signs of mental illness over the years. He said she attempted to commit suicide more than once. She even tried to physically harm women who she believed had affairs with him. One of them she tried to run over with a car. Fortunately, they paid her off so she wouldn't press charges. Another, she attacked in a beauty parlor, pinning the woman down on the floor and cutting off her hair with a scissor. They paid her off too. Terrence claims she did many insane and dangerous things, but attempting to kill Terrence is what really landed her at the hospital."

"Oh, my God."

"He has a stab wound in his shoulder. Michelle did it. It was an attempt on his life after a series of other things she did to him."

Moments later, Bryce showered. While Amara listened to the soothing sound of the water running, her thoughts drifted to Michelle and Terrence. The beautiful, vivacious woman who she had seen in the internet photos with Terrence hardly appeared like the dangerous woman that Terrence described her as. It all made Amara think about people. So many of them wore masks. Just because a person looked like they had it altogether, didn't mean that they did. Pondering about this, Terrence and Michelle, Amara's lids became heavy. Within seconds, she fell asleep. Suddenly she was somewhere else.

Beneath the vivid sunshine, Michelle walked along the manicured grounds of Terrence's estate. Guests were arriving for a party. She greeted them all and at the same time, she was looking nervously around for someone else. Then all of a sudden, everyone vanished. Nightfall replaced the lovely day. Michelle looked around at the sudden darkness and fear came over her face. She didn't start backing away until someone approached her. It was Terrence.

He held a knife and ran towards her. Michelle ran away, screaming. To her misfortune, he caught her. Then suddenly she couldn't be seen, only heard. There were only the sounds of her screams, piercing screams, until suddenly, there was silence.

When Bryce saw Terrence the next workday, he tried to keep his cool about Terrence's insults to Amara at the party. After all, Amara was concerned that if he defended her, Terrence would surely figure out Bryce and she were lovers. It was difficult to control his anger. More than once, Bryce was tempted to slam his fist in Terrence's mouth. Thinking about what Amara wanted restrained him. Still, when Bryce managed to wind up alone in Terrence's office, he had to say something.

"So man, why did you go off at the party like that?" He stood above Terrence's desk with his hands forcibly in his pockets.

Terrence searched his drawer for something. "What are you talking about?"

"I mean I heard you were rude to one of our employees."

Terrence's jaw tightened and he looked up. "Who?"

"Amara."

Terrence smiled coolly. "Man, I was drunk. You know how I get."

"They say a drunken mouth speaks a sober mind."

"It sure is the damn truth," Terrence agreed amusedly. "Hey man, what can I say? I want to hit it, you know that. And when I was drunk at the party, all of that nastiness easily came out of me."

Bryce sighed irritably. "Man, please don't do that again. We don't want her to wind up suing us."

"Suing us for what?" Terrence remained amused.

"Sexual harassment, of course."

"Ah, man, please. Everyone knows I had that sweet little pussy."

Bryce's heart did a leap, and it took all the strength he had to stop himself from jumping across the table and choking Terrence. Thinking of what Amara wanted, he kept his emotions in check and headed to the door, instead.

"Where you going?" Terrence asked with a stealthy smirk.

"I'm going back to work," Bryce shot, slamming the door.

Bryce and Amara strove to forget about Terrence as they spent time together the following weekend. Inside a room in his house that he had designated for his art, they set out to make fantasies come true. Amara wore a white, silky kimono with nothing underneath and let it drop to the floor. Bryce, seated behind his canvas and surrounded by numerous paint palettes and various sized brushes, sat frozen by her seductiveness.

"You're so beautiful, baby," he said, his eyes roaming over her naked curves.

"I feel beautiful when you look at me that way. Now, how would you like for me to pose?"

His twinkling eyes shifted to the nearby chaise. "Lie down on that and I'll do the rest."

Amara sprawled enticingly across the couch and gazed straight into his brown eyes. Bryce looked at her and made a few strokes across the canvas, before standing and walking towards her.

"What?" she asked, as he approached her. "You want to pose me a different way?"

"No, baby. I can't paint you like this. But I would like to use my tongue like a brush all over your body."

"You're nasty, Bryce," she cooed as he began to kiss her.

"And you like me that way," he said, through their crushing lips.

When they uncoupled, he stood and pulled off his t-shirt. When he came back down to her, his lips danced with hers again, before Amara felt the luscious assault of his tongue on hers. As he tasted her, she couldn't get enough, especially when he began to use his tongue just as he promised. Kissing, blowing, licking, he made an erotic brush with his mouth. First, he pampered each beautiful feature of her face, and then the thin skin along her neck. When he reached her breasts, Amara thrust her chest forward to give him complete access.

Bryce showed his appreciation by gliding his lips over her breasts while squeezing them, making her lower body soak with the need to feel him. Yet, he carried on his sweet torture, putting as much of her breasts as he could in his mouth and then sucking her nipples until they were ultra sensitive.

His love crusade continued with brushes of his lips and tongue down her belly. His tongue pressed firmly at the bottom of it where the stirrings of desire within her were almost unbearable. Then he went straight for her core. Positioning himself between her legs, he kissed the insides of her silky thighs, making a path straight to her vagina. There, his fingers thrust deep inside of her, making her whimper with delight. And just when she thought it couldn't feel any better, he traded his fingers for his tongue. In and out it went, like a hot speak inside her tight, wet place, and sought out her clit for the ultimate pleasure. He blew it. He kissed it. He sucked it. He licked it.

When neither of them could stand anymore without being one, Bryce stood and let her unzip his jeans and pull off his pants. His thick, long penis was so ready for her he could barely fit into the condom. Soon, she trembled as he put the tip of it inside her.

Amara's legs clamped around his waist and her arms hooked

around his neck. Bryce then pushed so deeply inside her that it seemed he would go through her, the fire burning up her flesh, assured her of their passionate fate.

At first, he moved at a snail's pace with an erotic movement all his own. Gliding her hips torridly with his, Amara had never known anything could feel so good. Tears of joy slipped from her eyes and she had no control of her trembling legs. Then, Bryce unleashed more from his hot arsenal. Fiercely, he pounded her. All the while he lapped up the juices from her mouth and licked everywhere on her body.

Feeling him thrusting wildly within her, Amara's body craved more and more of the intoxicating sensation. She clenched her muscles to hold him within her love forever. But soon out-of-this-world sensations overpowered each of them. Together their limbs shuddered. Their outcries saturated the air. Bryce collapsed on top of her, and both of them lay spent and soaked with sweat.

In a split second after making love, Bryce dozed off

Bryce's doorbell rang, waking both of them. Bryce glanced at the clock and realized they had slept for two hours. Wondering if it was Chris and his mother coming by, he pecked Amara on the cheek, hurried into his robe, and padded down the steps. Opening his front door, he was surprised to see his sister-in-law, Lynne. Before when she traveled in the area, she phoned. He was surprised that she would just drop by.

Bryce wanted to get back upstairs with Amara, but welcomed her in anyway. "How are you doing, sis?" He pecked her cheek.

Lynne gave him a tight hug and stepped into the house. "I'm real good, now that I see you."

Bryce thought she sounded a little too excited to see her mere brother-in-law. Then again, it was okay. He was a connection to someone she had loved dearly. They walked to the living room and he gestured for her to sit on the sofa.

"Have a seat."

Lynne didn't sit until he did, joining him on the loveseat.

"So your business has brought you near Crystal Falls again?"

Bryce asked.

"No, I was just thinking about you and I wanted to share something with you."

Lines dented his forehead with his curiosity. "Wow. It must be something serious for you to come all the way from Chicago."

"It is." Lynne faced him with a serious expression.

"So tell me." He noticed her eyeing his robe. Wondering if it was loose and showing a little too much of him, he tightened the belt. "You have me in suspense."

"There is something I have been feeling."

"What? Are you sick?" He searched her face, but she looked well and fit. "Please don't tell me that."

"Maybe. There is a possibility."

"Oh, no." Harshly he frowned.

"I may be love sick." She stared intensely in his eyes.

Bryce reared back in surprise. "Huh?"

"I think I'm in love with you, Bryce," she confessed and waited for his response.

However, instead of verbally reacting, Bryce sat speechless. He stared at her, then looked away, then stared at her again. Lynne couldn't have been saying this to him—not his beloved wife's sister. Yet she was. He had no clue she felt this way. He had not only thought of Lynne as Kimberly's sister, but his sister, too.

His lack of response made her look disappointed. "What do you say to that?"

Bryce thought for a moment. He didn't want to hurt her feelings, nor lead her on. "I think you may be confused, Lynne."

"No, I'm not. I've always had feelings for you. And I really don't think my family would be upset about it. They know you were so good to Kim, and they know you would be the same way with me."

Bryce shook his head in disbelief. "Lynne, I was married to your sister. It's not right, and I know your family wouldn't be happy."

"Forget them then." She eased closer to him. "We would be happy. I could make you happy. I could move in here." She clutched his hand. "I know you have women, but I know there is no one special. I feel this powerful chemistry between us."

"As two people who loved Kim."

"No, as two people who could love each other. I love you so much, enough for both of us. And I will treat you so good. I know in time, you will feel that way, too. Please let's try."

Just then, Amara, clad in her silky, white kimono, walked down the stairs. She smiled at Lynne and walked over to her, extending her hand.

"I'm Amara. We really didn't get introduced last time. Bryce has told me about your sister. It's nice to meet you."

Lynne looked lost and didn't even pretend that she wanted to shake Amara's hand. She gazed at Bryce. "This is serious?"

Amara stood back, looking astonished at her behavior. But Bryce, wanting everyone in the world to know how much he loved Amara, took her extended hand. "Lynne, Amara and I are in love."

Lynne looked down, shaking her head, and then stood. Her eyes grew teary and her lips quivered. She attempted to say something, but the words choked in her emotion. She hurried to the door and soon Bryce heard it slam.

Looking stunned, Amara swung around the sofa and sat on Bryce's lap. Slipping his arms around her, he shared what had just happened. He remained shocked, but Amara wasn't.

"I could tell she liked you when I saw her the first time."

He swayed back from her, surprised. "You could?"

"Sure. Women can sense these things about other women."

"Well I didn't have a clue. Not one. I just thought of her as my sister-in-law, and assumed she thought of me as just her brother-in-law."

"But she thought of you as much more. I'm not mad at her. In fact, I can't blame the woman. You're just too sexy." She kissed his lips and pulled him down on the couch with her.

He slipped his arms around her shoulders and they nestled close. "How about doing me a favor?"

She looked up at him. "Anything. What is it?"

"How about you leaving Jamie's place and get away from that Carlyn you're always complaining about and moving in here with me? I'll even try not to tell Terrence what's up until you're ready. We'll keep everything quiet. We'll move you in this week if you like."

"Oh, baby!" she threw her arms around his neck. "I would love to."

Amara returned to Jamie's place to grab her sexiest dress to go out dancing with Bryce. He had headed out to the grocer to get items to cook her a special celebration dinner about her moving in. So when she returned to his place, they would eat the scrumptious meal, and then go out and party.

Amara hurried to Jamie's room, yearning to share her good news with her friend. One peek inside, she noticed Jamie hadn't returned from her flight to California. She then continued to her own bedroom. Inside, she picked the red dress she had came for, but also a lovely turquoise one that she thought would look fabulous on the dance floor. Deciding to try them on, she took off her clothes.

When she heard the sound of the door opening, she swung around holding the dress in front of her, expecting to see Jamie. Instead, she saw Phil, the guy Carlyn was dating. When she first met him, Amara believed him to be a decent guy. Yet, as he drooled at her half-dressed and trying to hide herself, she knew better.

"Sugar, you look good," he said, "Maybe you need to join Carlyn and me in other room for some naughty fun."

"Get out!" Amara yelled. "Get out of my room!"

She shouted so loudly Carlyn ran down the hall to her bedroom door. Carlyn slapped Phil, making him get out of her way. Then she stepped toward Amara, shaking her hand.

"You touch me," Amara exclaimed, "and I'm not getting out of the way. It's on."

"You just can't stay away from other women's men, can you?"

"Look, missy, I was in my room, minding my own business. This creep walks in and says something lewd to me! Now, that's not my fault!"

"Oh, you act so innocent." Carlyn stepped close in her face, shaking her finger. "You're a slut if I've ever seen one!"

"Get out of my face! Get your finger out of my face! Get out of my room!" Amara shouted at the top of her lungs, still clutching the dress in front of her.

"Can't stand the truth, huh? Well, everybody knows. Everybody knows that you're doing Bryce, Terrence's best friend. Do you now switch up on the weekends?"

Amara's heart raced at her words. "What are you talking about?"

"About what I know. Elaine saw you two getting busy. You and Bryce! Doing you in his office. How tacky! Right under Terrence's nose. I'm surprised he hasn't wiped the floor with you two already. Because I just could not wait to tell him the good news!"

"What?"

"You heard me. I had dinner with Terrence and told him about you two. He was mad as hell."

"Well, let him get mad! Terrence is married! He is married!"

"That didn't stop you from opening your legs."

"You don't know what you're talking about!" Amara yelled, lunging at Carlyn, and shoving her out of the room with such force Carlyn could only stumble back. Once rid of the trash, Amara slammed the door shut and locked it. With shaky fingers, she dialed Bryce's home phone. When the answering service clicked on, she realized he must have still been out at the grocery store. For some reason, Terrence knowing about them and not saying anything terrified her. Bryce had to know what Carlyn had just told her. Without a doubt, Terrence wouldn't let them get away with it.

Inside his Mercedes-Benz, Bryce already felt like he was dancing in a nightclub. The only thing missing was his beautiful lady. As he bounced to an old school groove by R. Kelly, his dashboard lit up like stars surrounded by a moonlit sky. His stereo system was outstanding. The speakers boomed with the bass and drums. Overall, the music was so loud that he couldn't hear the ringer on his cell phone. Neither did he pay attention to see a telephone number light up its tiny screen.

What Bryce did notice inside his car, was an old vehicle that had driven behind him ever since he left the grocers. It had black tinted windows. Even when Bryce steered off the main highway to the lonesome road leading up to his home, the old car duplicated his actions.

Sensing that something wasn't right about the old car following him, Bryce slowed. The car slowed. Bryce sped up. The car sped up. Bryce then cut off the stereo and rolled his windows down. He waved, daring the driver to drive parallel with him. Instead, the driver charged behind him, crashing into his rear. The old car threw Bryce's vehicle out of control and bumped him off the road.

Not believing this was happening, Bryce steadied himself as his luxury vehicle tumbled into a ditch. His heart felt like it jumped in this throat and then sped out of control as he went down. When the car finally crashed, Bryce's forehead bashed against the steering wheel. Blood dripped from his nose as he managed to pry open the stuck driver's door.

Sore, bruised, and bloodied, he pulled himself out of the car and managed to crawl up on the ground. Hearing a car door slam, followed by footsteps, halted any further movements. The lunatic who ran him off the road approached. His face downward, Bryce feigned unconsciousness. He couldn't wait to see who had just tried to kill him.

Chapter Fourteen

At first, the footfalls were slow and then sped up as the unknown person stepped toward Bryce. At his side hidden from the attacker, Bryce balled his fist up. The person bent down to look in Bryce's face. Bryce raised his head and leveled his eyes with his attacker. Blood rose in his head when he faced Terrence.

Of all the people in the world to try to end his life, Bryce would have never imagined that it would be his best friend. Terrence and he were brothers in every sense--so he thought.

Bryce brought his fist up between Terrence's eyes so hard that Terrence stumbled backwards. Giving him no chance to gain his posture, he leaped on him and pounded. Before Bryce had time to think about anything, they were like mad animals out for blood, battling upon the dirt road. When Bryce saw blood spewing from Terrence's mouth and noticed that his friend was unable to get up, he stood back from him.

Shaking his head, Bryce shouted, "Why?"

Terrence raised his head, but still couldn't stand. "Because you're a dirty son of a bitch!"

"I asked you why."

"Why? Why? Why do think?" Terrence shouted back at him. "You think you could screw her and I not find out about it? You little punk, you were so scared to tell me, because you knew I would blow your ass off this earth!" Terrence spit blood from his mouth near Bryce's shoes.

"No, I didn't tell you, because of Amara. She worried about

the friendship and partnership I had with you, and she had this crazy idea you could be dangerously vengeful. Now, I know she had every right to feel that way. You're sick, Terrence!" He shook his head, still amazed at what his old friend tried to do to him. "You're the one who needs help, not Michelle!"

"Whatever I am, my friend," Terrence said between gritted teeth, "I am no longer in partnership with you. My lawyer will contact you. And believe me you'd better be ready, because we plan to eat you alive."

"Bring it on."

With that, Bryce limped away from the crash site, leaving bleeding Terrence lying on the dirt.

By the time Amara arrived at Bryce's house, he stood in the bedroom, patching up his wounds. When he recounted what happened, she felt hysterical. Though, she knew she needed to remain calm to help him. Since Bryce refused to go to the hospital to see if he was seriously injured, she made him sit on the bed so she could take care of his injuries as best she could.

There was a bad bruise and bump on his forehead. He also had scrapes on his arms and a small cut on his leg. Carefully Amara cleaned wounds, rubbed alcohol over abrasions and applied Vaseline and peroxide to areas of his body that needed it. After she bandaged him all the areas, she pressed Bryce to tell her more about what happened.

Devastated, he didn't want to discuss the ordeal any longer. As Amara stood above him, he put his arms around her and laid his head against her stomach. Looking down at him, she stroked his head. He reminded her of a sad boy. In the silence, she could almost hear his thoughts. His best friend, Terrence Johnson, had actually tried to take his life.

The next day, Amara was grateful that Bryce was back to his old self. She accompanied him to the police station to press charges against Terrence and was proud of how undaunted he was when the authorities paid Terrence a visit and he convinced them that it was an accident. Bryce was determined to make him pay in other ways.

When they returned home, they sat on the patio, enjoying a nice meal and a meeting of the minds. It resulted in Bryce scheduling a meeting in the afternoon with his attorney to begin the process of severing his business ties with Terrence. He had also scheduled a meeting with a business consultant to set up a new real estate firm, of which Amara and he would run the firm as partners.

"I'm so sorry about what he tried to do to you," Amara said, as they settled down from all of their activities. She walked around to his side of the table and gently massaged his shoulders.

"Let's not talk about this anymore." He reached back for her and eased her down on his lap. "Now we're free to show our love and now we're going to be business partners."

Amara flashed him a sexy smile. "Wow. It does sound exciting. Why don't we go celebrate?"

"Whatever you want to do, baby."

Inside the house, Bryce backed Amara against the living room wall. The instant his lips melted into hers, his hand reached underneath her blouse. The twofold pleasure of his mouth and caress sent warmth racing down to her feminine core. Amara clasped her arms around his neck, relishing the smooth, luscious feel of his lips, and his scent. She drank in a potpourri of coconut oil and a woodsy-smelling cologne.

His tongue invading the honey inside her mouth was even more a succulent gift. While it danced greedily with hers, she felt Bryce's fingers exploding inside her bra, thumbing her nipples. Moistness and pulsations grew between her legs. Wild, erotic fire spread all through her.

In no time, Bryce led her to his bedroom. Once they stood by the tall, wood posts, he stared down at her body.

"I can't get enough of you."

"I can't get enough of you, either," Amara answered back.

Bryce drew Amara within his arms, holding her close against his body. "Do you feel that?" he whispered, writhing his hard, excited body against her. "Do you feel what you do to me?"

"Yes," Amara said, her voice drowning within his mouth as he kissed her.

Amara's heart raced as she tasted his love juices and as they undressed each other. At each glint of her bare flesh exposed to him, she saw the hunger growing in his eyes. She loved that she turned him on so much. When she finally had him out of his clothes, his muscular body and huge erection started a soaking, wet fire within her. It made her even hotter as she put a condom on him.

Amara lay back on Bryce's bed, unable to take her eyes off of him. As his eyes lingered in hers, he laid down beside her. Leaning over her, he kissed her hungrily while his hands roamed over her body. He lingered at her breasts, squeezing them and playing with her nipples until she whimpered for more. In his eagerness to please, his mouth traded places with his fingers. He sucked her breasts and nipples until Amara squirmed from the sinful delight of his hot mouth. Then doubling her ecstasy, he reached down between her legs.

He slipped his finger within her silky patch. With it, he teased her with erotic motions, giving her a taste of what was to come. Moaning for more, Amara gripped his hard, long love. "Please baby, please give it me. I need it. Put it deep in me."

At last, Bryce sat between her legs, moving them apart with his thighs. He caressed her tight silkiness once more, and then guided his steel-hard penis inside of her. The shock of feeling him pushing so deep inside of her thrilled Amara so much, she trembled. Holding on to his back, she also began to move with him.

His buried his head into the crook of her neck. Fiercely, he moved in and out of her. The rapture sent Amara spinning, her limbs thrashing. He reached under grabbing her buttocks, deepening his thrusts and groaning as if he couldn't get enough. The pleasure swirling inside Amara squeezed tears from her eyes and made her scream. She held on tighter to Bryce's sweaty back, giving all that she had to give. She swung her hips so erotically that his groans rivaled her screams. And when she felt her senses exploding with the rush that neither could control, her body shuddered and she called out his name loudly.

They fell asleep and when they awakened, they ate, and made love again. They enjoyed themselves in the kitchen a few times and eventually, their ravenous appetite for each other led them to a blanket on the living room floor. Before long, Amara felt Bryce inside of her again, stroking her silky walls. Unable to get enough of him, she moved her hips to his erotic rhythm, drawing out every drop of pleasure. Before long, they climaxed and lay limp and spent again.

Bryce had just felt him himself succumbing to his body's exhaustion and falling asleep when the phone rang. It woke Amara, as well. Both sat up when he picked up the receiver.

"Hello?"

"Bryce?" a woman cried. "Bryce, please help me."

Slowly he recognized the voice. "Michelle?"

"Yes, it's me. Terrence is really is trying to kill me. Please, you have to help me. I have no one else."

Bryce thought for only a moment. If Terrence was capable of killing him, he was also capable of killing his wife. "Michelle, don't worry. I'll be there. Just give me the name of your facility and I'll do the rest."

Bryce packed for North Carolina in preparation for visiting Michelle. Amara begged to go with him. However, since he didn't know what type of perilous situation he was headed for he left her at his home, with a bodyguard. He suspected Terrence would try to get back at Amara. He didn't know how, but he didn't want to risk any chances with her safety.

"Now, Steve is here for your safety" Bryce told Amara. "As soon as I come back, we won't need him. But while you're here alone, it's best that he is here. I don't trust Terrence after what he did to me. If you suspect anything awry, you let Steve know."

"I will." She nodded and gazed at him sadly.

"He's the best in the business," he added, hating that he had to leave her. Yet he couldn't let Terrence harm Michelle. "He will always be posted outside."

"Sure." She smiled, but it quickly faded.

Silently Bryce stared at her. With every item that he placed in the suitcase, she looked more and more distressed. "Baby, it's going to be all right." He threw the items aside and stepped close to her.

Amara brought her arms around his shoulders. "I know it will."

"I love you. And I'm coming back to you. And we're going to be so happy." He closed in on her lips and kissed her until his body grew rock hard.

Chapter Fifteen

When Michelle saw Bryce enter her room, she felt so relieved that tears filled her eyes. With her father having passed on, and Terrence convincing her friends that she was too insane to see anyone, it meant everything that Bryce came. But not only had he come, he had come to rescue her.

Sitting on the bed beside her, Bryce grasped her hand. "First off, I didn't believe at first Terrence was capable of murder. But, I surely believe it now."

"What changed your mind?" Michelle asked.

"He tried to kill me."

Michelle's hand covered her mouth. "You? You're his best friend and partner."

Bryce looked off, thinking of the nightmare he had endured. It still turned his stomach when he thought about Terrence attempting to murder him. He focused back on Michelle. "Yes, he did it."

"Why? Because of a woman?"

Bryce hesitated in light of the sensitive situation. "He…"

"He wants her," Michelle finished Bryce's sentence. "I'm not surprised. He cheated on me like crazy, but I didn't know until it was too late. I loved him so much that when my dad died, I wanted to share that huge inheritance with him. I made the arrangements and we would share the fortune within the month. But I learned about him cheating on me with all these women and that he really didn't love me. I had an appointment to meet with my attorney to change it. I was advised that

I could do this up to a certain period of time.

"That's when he set me up as if I did all these crazy things to harm him and declared that I was incompetent to handle my finances or make important decisions. He spiked my drinks so I couldn't remember important things I had to do. And the stabbing, I recall being drugged and faintly remember him forcing my hand on the knife and making me stab him. But a regular shrink would have figured out his game. Terrence hooked me up with his crooked friend, Richard Hayes, who became the medical director here. They are in it together."

"In what together?"

"Drugging me with something that is supposed to ultimately kill me." A tear fell from her eye and she dabbed it with her finger. "But when they found out I wasn't swallowing the poisoned pills, they started to inject me with the drug. They didn't want me to have visitors. I bet they were shocked to see somebody finally came to visit me."

Bryce nodded. "In fact they were. They tried to discourage me, telling me how dangerous you were. But that didn't stop me. But don't you worry, you'll be out today."

Bryce had a fraternity brother, who was a detective in the police department in the area. When he visited Joesive Godfrey at his office, the two men briefly caught up on each other's lives before getting to the matter that brought Bryce to the stationhouse.

"So they are poisoning this woman?" Joesive asked, scratching his prematurely balding head.

Bryce nodded. "I wouldn't get you involved unless I knew this woman was in danger. Terrence Johnson tried to kill me, and now he's trying to kill his wife."

Within hours of meeting with Bryce, Godfrey and his partner interrogated Richard Hayes, the medical director of the Briarwood Psychiatric Hospital. Nervously Hayes lied until Godfrey's questions became so clever that he could no longer hide the truth. In exchange for a lighter prison sentence, he shared Terrence's scheme with the police.

Richard confessed they had teamed up because Terrence's wife wanted to reclaim the sizable inheritance that she had signed papers to share with him. Terrence learned that she had a good chance legally of things going in her favor and he wasn't going to allow that to happen. By any means necessary, he wanted to get rid of Michelle.

He went to drastic measures to have her declared insane. After she was committed, he learned of a new, black market drug, which would slowly kill her. Many coroners didn't even know about it and weren't testing for it. Terrence wouldn't be connected to the murder. It would be attributed to an unknown medical cause. After Michelle's death, Terrence would never have to worry about the inheritance. Michelle would never be able to fight him in court about it. Moreover, not half, but all of it would belong to him.

That evening in Crystal Falls, Terrence sat at his desk in TJ Realty, still seething about Amara and Bryce's betrayal. Comforting himself with alcohol, he reached for a glass of vodka and took several swigs. When he sat the half-empty glass back down, he was startled to hear the phone ring. Angrily, he swiped up the receiver.

"Hello."

"Hello yourself, sweetie pie," a woman greeted him with a chuckle.

Recognizing Michelle's voice, Terrence sat up. "What are you doing calling me?"

"I just wanted to let you know that I'm free," she practically sang.

Terrence glowered and thought. Richard wouldn't have let her out. Had she escaped again? "What the hell are you talking about?" he demanded.

"That I'm free, free, free! I'm not locked up so you can kill me. Your sweet friend helped me. I'm on my way to see my family and friends, and you can't stop me now. Then I'm going to see my lawyer and make sure you're bankrupt!"

Terrence stood. "So, you were successful in getting away this time. I'm going to call the authorities."

"Be careful there, dear. They've already been called on you

first."

"What?" he shot, trying not to let her upset him. But he couldn't stop his heart from racing out of control. "What is this crazy talk about?"

"I'm not crazy!" Michelle shouted. "I'm saner than you. You're the nut! You tried to kill me and then you tried to kill Bryce."

Terrence loosened his necktie and tried to calm his nerves. "Who told you about Bryce?"

"He did. He came to see me. He got me out of there. He got to the bottom of your murder scheme and your criminal friend spilled his guts to the police. So, you don't have to call the authorities. They are coming to you, lover boy!"

Click.

Frantic with worry, Terrence locked up the business and headed home. Before he drove closer to his estate, he saw several police cars with their lights blinking speeding towards his home. Doing an immediate U-turn, he sped off in the opposite direction.

When Bryce returned home after rescuing Michelle from her situation, Amara felt in love with him more than ever. She longed to show him her appreciation and thought a strip show might titillate him. Hence, she took off every stitch of clothing like a stripper.

Bryce licked his lips and his dark, sparkling eyes glistened with that I'm-going-to-tear-you-up look. Hungry for his delicious hot love, she swung her hips provocatively until she reached the bed. Bryce shifted, sitting up on the side of the mattress. She backed up on his lap and felt his huge erection pressing into her bottom.

"That's it, baby. All this is for you," he whispered, pressing his lips against Amara's ear.

His breathing became heavy as he reached around squeezing her breasts so much and anxiously, as if he expected juice to come out. Then he heightened his foreplay, stroking one of her nipples ever so slowly while the other hand reached between her thighs and teased her love until it pulsated. She became so super moist and excited she whimpered and begged Bryce for the love he pushed against her bottom.

He acquiesced by kissing her neck with such heavenly delight she rolled her head back toward his shoulders. A breath later, he swung her around and lay Amara on the bed. He buried his head between her thighs and tongued her love as no other man ever could. She indulged him with same luscious treatment and he had to force himself not to come in reaction to her moves. She relished the taste of his honeyed tongue and lapped up the juiciness of his soft lips.

But her body ached for more and so did his. They kissed until neither could withstand the sweet torture of not being one. He moved between her legs and spread them apart. Soon, she welcomed him inside of her and moaned from the pleasure of feeling every inch of him.

Bryce kissed her. Deep, greedy kisses exploded her senses as hotly as the wild strokes he ravished her with. Sweat poured from his body in an instant. She licked it and tasted every drop while moving and clenching her feminine muscles to hold him tight. She made him groan as if the ecstasy was unbearable.

Amara couldn't get enough of him. Just when the orgasm had her spinning, he drew out the pleasure longer. Getting into a new position, Bryce threw her legs over his shoulders. As he tantalized her with beastly in and out thrusts that felt so unbearably good, Amara never wanted it to end, his eyes whispered how much he loved her. She felt his love as she felt the excitement, which soon sent her body and his shuddering out of control.

Afterward they basked in the afterglow of love until Amara felt the need for a shower. Slipping on her sexy, white kimono, she walked towards Bryce's bathroom. When she noticed there was a problem with the showerhead in his bathroom, she stepped down the hall to another bathroom. Just as she stepped inside of the hallway bathroom, a hand came from behind and covered her mouth, muffling her screams.

Chapter Sixteen

Bryce lay in bed with his hands behind his head, reliving the sexy time he had just experienced with Amara. Suddenly he heard noises, miscellaneous bumping, and then a muffled scream. Rushing out into the hall, it appeared empty. Yet when he moved further out so that he had a better view, he saw Terrence, covering Amara's mouth, and trying to drag her down the steps.

Bryce ran toward him. Just as he reached him, Terrence pulled out a knife. Swiftly he placed it beneath Amara's neck. "I'll kill her! If she's not running away with me, she's damn sure not staying here with you. She was my woman!" Terrence had a crazy wild-eyed look on his face.

Bryce eased towards him with baby steps. "Let her go, man. Please, let her go!"

"Why would I do that, so you two can live happily ever after? Man, you fucked my life! You took everything from me, my fortune, my freedom and now my woman!" Terrence continued to hold the knife at Amara's neck. She looked at Bryce, crying and trembling.

"No Terrence, you took them all away," Bryce tried to reason with him. "You tried to kill your wife for money, for greed. You lied to Amara and tried to destroy her, too."

Bryce noticed that while they exchanged words, Terrence moved the knife away from Amara's throat. When it seemed to be at a distance that wouldn't cause her harm, Bryce lunged. They wrapped together and tussled. Amara screamed and ran to the telephone. By the time the 911 operator came on the line, Terrence had tumbled down the stairs and he lay unconscious at the bottom.

The ambulance and authorities arrived. Terrence was escorted from Bryce's house on a stretcher, handcuffed. A police officer rode with him in the ambulance. Amara sighed with relief realizing all the problems they had with Terrence were now finally over. Tears of released tension glistened in her eyes.

Hours later, on the sofa, Bryce pulled Amara within his arms. With the first press of his lips slowly grinding into hers, a lusty ache grew within her. The tantalizing sensation escalated as their hunger deepened. She parted her lips allowing him access to her honey. She eased backward, allowing him to access to love her all over.

Savoring the erotic taste of him, Amara soon felt his hands everywhere on her body. With it, he eased her out of her clothes. Before long, she lied naked on the couch. Bryce's breaths rasped loud and thick, as his eyes devoured her. Feeling sexy and beautiful because of the way he gazed at her, Amara soon felt his kisses all over. When he concentrated on her nipples flicking his tongue on them, his fingers squeezed her entire breasts. Amara lost her mind from the pleasure she was receiving.

Bryce removed his shirt, pants, shorts, and Amara thrilled him with her magical way of putting on a condom. Soon, he lay on top of her and guided his long, thick, erect penis within her tight walls. She whimpered and put her arms around him, holding on tight. As she did, her stomach muscles clenched. From the feeling of him penetrating her deeper, her love soaked from the joy of the sweet invasion of him again and again.

Bryce gripped her buttocks and arched his body to move in and out slowly. Amara's hips matched his motions. She welcomed the hot sensations that only Bryce could unleash on her. As their passion increased, so did his speed. Dripping sweat, his face frowned as if in pain and he pumped with the fierceness of a starving man greedily consuming his last meal. Then all too soon, they felt themselves spinning off the cliff of rapture of which they had no control. Her limbs shuddering, Amara gazed in Bryce's eyes. He gazed in hers.

"Will you marry me?" he asked.

"Oh, baby, yes, yes."

About the Author

Louré Bussey began her career writing romance stories for magazines. After spending one summer penning her first novel, she was ecstatic when an editor offered her a two-book contract. Now, a best-selling author of thirteen novels, her steamy, thrilling page-turners are highly acclaimed by readers and reviewers. Her other successes include screenwriting, a forthcoming music CD "Dreams Do Come True" and a fashion line.

Parker Publishing, LLC

Celebrating Black
Love Life Literature

Mail or fax orders to:
12523 Limonite Avenue Suite #440-438
Mira Loma, CA 91752
phone: (866) 205-7902 fax: (951) 685-8036 fax
or order from our Web site: www.parker-publishing.com

orders@parker-publishing.com

Ship to:

Name: _____

Address: _____

_____

City: _____

State: _____ Zip:_____

Phone: _____

Qty	Title	Price	Total

Shipping and handling is $3.50, Priority Mail shipping is $6.00 FREE standard shipping for orders over $30

Add S&H Alaska, Hawaii, and international orders – call for rates

CA residents add 7.75% sales tax

Payment methods: We accept Visa, MasterCard, Discovery, or money orders.
NO PERSONAL CHECKS.

Payment Method: (circle one): VISA MC DISC Money Order

Name on Card: _____

Card Number: _____ ____

ExpDate: _____

Address: _____

_____

City: _____

State: _____ Zip:_____